BAKER'S DOZEN

AND THE WINNER IS...

Created by Miriam Zakon
Written by Aidel Stein

MENUCHA PUBLISHERS

Menucha Publishers, Inc.
First published 1992
© 2018 by Menucha Publishers
All rights reserved

ISBN 978-1-61465-553-4
Library of Congress Control Number: 2017916860

Published and distributed by:
Menucha Publishers, Inc.
1235 38th Street
Brooklyn, NY 11218
Tel/Fax: 718-232-0856
www.menuchapublishers.com
sales@menuchapublishers.com

Printed in Israel

BAKER'S DOZEN

AND THE WINNER IS...

Contents

WHO'S WHO IN THE BAKER'S DOZEN

ASHER BAKER, *age 16. The eldest of the Baker clan, Ashi dorms in a nearby yeshivah — but still manages to take part in the family's adventures!*

BRACHA BAKER, *age 13. It's not easy being the oldest girl in such a large family, especially when you've got five famous sisters just two years younger than you are! But Bracha always rises to the challenge, usually with a smile. Her hobbies are reading, gardening (with her mother), and painting.*

RIVKA BAKER, *age 11. Eldest of the quintuplets, Rivka often tries to mother — and sometimes tries to boss around — her sisters. A talented guitar player with a beautiful voice.*

ZAHAVA BAKER, *age 11. With eleven brothers and sisters, Zahava still manages to get her way. A pretty girl, the kind who gets picked to play Queen Esther in Purim plays, she is usually good-natured, but sometimes high-strung. Her hobbies are drawing, fashion, and needlepoint.*

DINA BAKER, *age 11. Dini is as dependable as her sister Zahava is flighty. She hates injustice and defends the underdog in any fight. Her hobbies include reading and dancing.*

TIKVA BAKER, *age 11. Tikva is blind in one eye and has very poor eyesight in the other; still, she is fiercely independent. Though she cannot see at all in the dark, she refuses to walk with a cane. A very bright girl, she reads all her books in braille. She is shy and reserved with strangers, but at home everyone looks to her for advice and support. Tikva writes poetry in her spare time.*

YOCHEVED BAKER, *age 11.* "The Baby Dynamo," *as her father calls her, is the smallest of the quints, and a ball of energy and excitement. Yochie's always ready for adventure, quick to anger but quick to forgive. She loves schemes, the more outrageous the better, but rarely thinks about consequences until she's up to her neck in them. Her hobbies change with every new month.*

MOISHY BAKER, *age 9.* "He's his father's genius, and my gray hairs," *is the way Mrs. Baker describes her difficult prodigy. When he's in the mood, he can memorize hundreds of mishnayos; when he doesn't feel like it, he can fail every math test his teacher gives him. He collects coins and is a computer whiz.*

CHEZKY BAKER, *age 8. A jolly boy, always laughing, terrible in his studies but so good-natured about it that even his teachers have to smile. An expert softball player.*

DONNY BAKER, *age 5. A tough cookie, an independent kid who doesn't care what anyone else thinks of him.*

SARALEH BAKER, *age 3. A sweet little girl, with a dangerous tendency to wandering off.*

RACHEL AHUVA BAKER, *age 1. A fat baby, all cheeks and tummy and legs. She's usually smiling — and why not, with four fathers and seven mothers (besides Abba and Ima)?*

1

Bracha's Blues

I can't believe I'm getting braces!" Zahava Baker said for what seemed to be the hundredth time. She leaned toward the mirror and bared her teeth in an exaggerated grimace at her reflection. "I don't think I can stand it!" As the prettiest of the eleven-year-old Baker quintuplets, Zahava spent a lot of time smiling at herself in the mirror.

Yochie, the most mischievous of the quints, came and stood next to her taller sister. "Don't worry, Zahava," Yochie said, tilting up her head to grin at her sister's reflection. "With all that silver in your mouth, your smile will be even more dazzling!"

Their younger brothers Chezky, eight, and Donny, five, an appreciative audience, chortled from Yochie's bed where they were watching the performance.

The Baker household, with its twelve children, sometimes seemed to be overtaken by the quints. Although each one had her own distinctive personality, as a group they often seemed to be at center stage.

"Oh, *ha*! Very *ha*," Zahava retorted. She picked up a brush and ran it vigorously through her hair. "You just wait till you get yours."

"Really, guys," said Dini, third of the quints and the one with the most active conscience. "Leave Zahava alone."

"I'm glad we don't have to have those molds taken of our mouths again," Rivka shuddered. "That was gross." The oldest quint by a few minutes — and the bossiest — Rivka turned around and made a rapid inspection. "Your hair doesn't look brushed, Yochie. Dini, your belt's on crooked. Tikva, do you want me to help you out?" She moved helpfully toward her sight-impaired sister, but Tikva only smiled and shook her head. Blind in one eye and having only partial vision in the other, Tikva wore thick glasses and a contented expression. She was the most good-natured of the five.

Rivka's ever-watchful eye caught sight of her brothers perched on Yochie's bed. Chezky — who, when he wasn't getting into trouble with Yochie, was almost as fond of relaxing as he was of softball — was sprawled full-length across the bedspread while Donny used his brother's stomach for a pillow.

"Chezky and Donny, get your feet off that bed this instant!"

The boys grumbled and grimaced but reluctantly complied. Zahava pulled a hideous face in the mirror, just as Moishy walked into the room.

"What's going on?" asked the nine-year-old near-genius.

"We've got a five-in-one deal at the orthodontist," Yochie told him. She turned to the boys on her bed. "Don't worry, guys. Maybe by accident they'll wire Rivka's mouth shut!"

The boys hooted. Zahava snorted. Tikva put her hand up over her mouth to stifle a laugh.

"Yochie!" Dini and Rivka snapped in unison.

"We'll give her a sign to wear around her neck," Chezky giggled. "Temporarily under Construction." He and Donny leaned back on the bed, kicking their legs and laughing uproariously.

"I always thought that braces looked like the inside of a radio," Moishy said thoughtfully. "I'll bet if you stand at the right angle and open your mouth, you might even be able to get shortwave."

"We could tune into Europe," Chezky put in excitedly. "Maybe even the Voice of Israel!"

"Train tracks!" offered Donny. "They look like train tracks!"

Yochie peered into Rivka's mouth. "Here comes the early late express!"

"YOCHIE!" Everyone else was in hysterics, but Dini and Rivka were indignant.

Moishy hopped over to the door. " 'Brace' yourselves,"

he called out with a wink. "Ima's coming!"

"OOOOOOOOOOH!" everyone groaned. A pillow flew toward the doorway. Moishy ducked, and the pillow narrowly missed Mrs. Baker.

"Oops," exclaimed Rivka, running to retrieve the pillow. "Sorry, Ima. That was meant for Moishy." She rolled her eyes. "Talk about bad puns...."

"I'd say it's more a question of bad aim," Chezky remarked.

"What's the story, kids?" Mrs. Baker asked. "Are all of you ready to go?" She shook her car keys meaningfully at the children. "There's no reason to be late."

"We'll be down in a jiffy," Tikva assured her mother.

"Just as soon as Zahava finishes admiring herself in the mirror," Yochie added merrily. She ducked as another pillow sailed through the air, this time aimed at her.

Mrs. Baker turned for the door with a brief "No nonsense now, kids." Over her shoulder she added, "I'll meet all of you at the car — in two minutes flat."

Rivka stalked after her. At the door she stopped and said stiffly, "All of you are lucky that I don't want to speak *lashon hara*."

"Oh, Rivka, I'm sorry," Yochie exclaimed, following her sister. "Don't be mad."

"Rivka's right," Dini scolded. "I don't think people should speak before they think."

"You're absolutely right," Yochie nodded. She turned back to Rivka. "Friends?"

Rivka considered her a minute. "Okay," she said. "Friends."

"Good!" said Yochie. She grinned up at her sister. "After all, we radios ought to stick together!"

"*Yochie!*"

The quints left. The performance over, Chezky and Donny went to their room, Donny shuffling his feet and making quiet train noises to himself.

Bracha, at thirteen the eldest Baker daughter, had been sitting quietly all this time while her sisters fooled around. She watched the last of them leave. The room seemed suddenly very quiet. She got up, intending to return to her room to study. But standing in the upstairs hall, she had a sudden impulse. Quickly, she ran down the stairs and looked for her mother.

She found her bundling the baby, Rachel Ahuva, into her snowsuit.

"Ima," she asked breathlessly, "can I come along?"

Mrs. Baker was surprised. "What for? Your appointment isn't until next week."

"I know," Bracha replied. "I just want to come along for the ride."

"In this weather? It's freezing out."

Bracha shrugged. "Why not?"

"All right, then. Hurry up and get in the car."

Hefting the baby, the bulging baby bag and her own pocketbook, Mrs. Baker walked out the front door. Bracha went to get her coat.

The front hall closet was a jumbled mess, as usual. The floor was covered with a mix-up of boots, balls, and bags, with an occasional glove that had fallen from someone's pocket. *Why isn't Yochie wearing her boots?* Bracha wondered as she put on her coat. *And who took my hat?*

She had no time to search for it. From outside came the tooting of the car's horn. Bracha bolted out of the door, pulling on her gloves as she went.

She slid into the front seat next to her mother — the oldest child's privilege. Buckling her seat belt, she half turned to glance at her sisters. Even with just six of them in the car — exactly one-half of the Baker brood — the car seemed crowded.

"Zahava," she demanded, "what are you doing with my hat?"

Zahava looked guilty. "I couldn't find mine," she confessed.

"You could have asked. I probably would have loaned it to you...."

"She's got a point," Mrs. Baker said, starting the car.

"I'm sorry," said Zahava. Reluctantly, she began to take it off. "I think it matches *my* coat better, actually."

"Oh, don't bother," said Bracha. "I'll use my hood."

Zahava brightened noticeably. "Thanks, Bracha!"

"No problem. Just ask next time."

Bracha turned around again and stared out the front window. *Zahava's right*, she thought. *The hat does look better on her.* She sighed, feeling suddenly very plain. Plain and boring. She often felt that way in the company of her five sisters. The quints were special just by being who they were. Bracha had to try harder.

It wasn't that she wanted to be noticed for her looks, especially. But it would be nice to be noticed for *something....*

It was drizzling lightly. The temperature hovered just above freezing, but a nasty wind made it feel much colder. Gray clouds covered the sky, blocking out all color. Not only was the sky overcast, but the ground looked overcast, too.

"I wish it would snow," Dini declared from the back seat.

There was a chorus of agreement from the rest of the passengers.

"What's the use of winter without snowball fights?" Yochie agreed. The car slowed as Mrs. Baker pulled into the parking lot of the West Bloomfield Medical Center. She found a space with little difficulty.

"Not so crowded today," she remarked. "We can thank the weather for that."

"Do you really think anyone would cancel an appointment just because it's raining?" Tikva asked her.

"They would if they were sick," Rivka said.

"But the main reason to have a doctor's appointment is being sick," objected Dini.

"The main reason we're here," Mrs. Baker reminded them all, "is to get you girls some braces. Let's go."

They ran through the parking lot in the rain. The waiting room of the Medical Center was like a warm haven after the gloomy outdoors. Bracha had always liked the decor. The walls were yellow and orange, and full of all sorts of pictures relevant to dentistry. There were plants everywhere. She had read somewhere that plants had a soothing effect. Patients in a dentist's waiting room could probably use all the soothing they could get.

The receptionist, a cheerful middle-aged woman named Mrs. Willis, looked up at the commotion as the Bakers trooped in. "Well, hello there!" she greeted them. "If it isn't Mrs. Baker and her five look-alikes!"

This wasn't strictly true; the quintuplets didn't look any more alike than most sisters do. But Mrs. Willis didn't worry about accuracy as she gushed over the five eleven-year-olds. The people waiting on the striped couches listened and stared and smiled.

Bracha stood to one side during the grand reception. *I've been coming here for a year and no one ever brought out the brass band for* me, she reflected. But then, everything that involved the quints always became a major production.

Bracha took a seat in a corner of the room. Sitting there, she felt about as noticeable as one of the potted plants that lined the walls. Why, she wondered, had she asked to come along, anyway? She wasn't sure. It wasn't as if she actually enjoyed going to the orthodontist. She hadn't finished studying for tomorrow's test yet. Besides, she had to be back here again next week for her own appointment. Really, this was kind of a waste of time.

Then she saw the answer. It was staring her right in the face.

All she'd really wanted, she decided with a pang, was to be a part of things. She was so tired of always feeling left out....

2

On the Sidelines

To pass the time, Bracha got up and wandered over to the case where the molds of the patients' teeth were displayed.

The quintuplets had been given a shelf of their own. A sign glued to the rim of the shelf proclaimed: THE BAKER QUINTUPLETS — BEFORE. Her own mold was lower down, with her name on a much smaller card: "Bracha Baker — before."

As she studied the array of teeth, she thought of each of her sisters in turn.

First came Rivka. *My main competition*, she joked to herself. *Actually, she's the most like me. We're both very responsible — the "take charge" types. That's good; a big family like ours needs that.*

But sometimes she really gets in my way. After all, I am the oldest....

Yochie was sitting next to Rivka. She sat with her legs crossed, swinging one foot back and forth. Those two were so different, you almost wouldn't think they were sisters. Bracha smiled to herself. *Rivka's always making up rules — and Yochie's always trying to wriggle out of them!*

The dental assistant came into the room. "Zahava?" she called.

With a last forlorn smile at her family, Zahava left the waiting room for the orthodontist's chair.

Bracha watched her go. *None of us Bakers is bad-looking,* she thought, *but Zahava's something special. It's just a pity she knows it....*

Dini came out of the inner office. Her mouth looked uncomfortable. It was funny how she and Zahava were the only ones who looked almost like twins. Bracha thought back on the scene in the quints' room earlier. *Good for her, telling Yochie off like that. Trust Dini to remember where the limits were.* Even though Bracha herself couldn't resist a secret smile at the jokes....

When it was Tikva's turn to see the orthodontist, Yochie accompanied her in. *Yochie is the only one of us who manages to help Tikva without making it look like help,* Bracha thought, with a twinge of admiration. Poor Tikva — thick glasses *and* braces. *Well, she doesn't feel sorry for herself. I won't give her pity that she doesn't want or need.*

"Bracha?" Startled out of her thoughts, Bracha looked up — straight into her mother's eyes. She blinked.

"Wake up!" her mother said briskly. "Since you're already here I asked the doctor to see you now so you won't have to come back next week. Come."

Bracha climbed into the chair, feeling very much like an afterthought. As Mrs. Baker and the orthodontist chatted about the quints, Bracha once again marveled at her mother with her simple but attractive way of dressing. Bracha rarely remembered seeing her without a baby on her arm — as she held Rachel Ahuva now. People, she knew, often wondered how her mother managed, and how she almost always kept her cool. She made having twelve kids look almost easy!

Lost in her reflections, she didn't realize the orthodontist had finished with her until she heard his final, "We're all through here." She hopped off the chair.

As the children struggled into their bulky winter coats and scarves and hats, Mrs. Baker lingered at the receptionist's desk to set up appointments for the next time. With Mrs. Willis's cheery good-byes following them, they went out to the car.

It was raining harder now. Bracha shivered as she buckled the baby into her car seat, and then took her own place up front.

"Now for the birthday party!" Zahava squealed happily. She bounced twice in her seat.

"Yay!" echoed Dini, bouncing, too.

"Double yay!" said Yochie. She bounced even higher.

"Triple yay!" said Zahava, beginning to match her.

"Oh no, you don't!" warned Mrs. Baker. "The shocks can't take this!" As the girls settled down, she glanced at Bracha, beside her. "Bracha, will you watch the younger kids while I drive the girls to their party?"

"Whose birthday is it?" Bracha asked curiously.

"A new girl in our class — you don't know her," Zahava told her.

"Once I'm out in the car, I'll probably run a few errands, too," Ima continued. "Okay, Bracha?"

Bracha slouched slightly in her seat. "Sure, Ima, no problem. I'll babysit." She concentrated on making herself sound eager and helpful.

Back home, she took charge of the baby while her mother started supper in the kitchen and the quints went to their room to change into their party clothes. Rachel Ahuva was soon sleeping soundly, her cheeks still pink from the cold. Bracha watched her a moment and then slipped out. She followed the noise to the quints' room.

As usual, Zahava's bed was piled high with clothes, dresses she had tried on and then discarded. She'd finally settled on one, and was busy searching for the perfect headband to wear with it. Dini was finished dressing and was helping Tikva find a ribbon to match her dress. Rivka, also ready, kept reminding her sisters of the time, while Yochie hopped from one sister to another, begging for a pair of matching socks.

Watching them, Bracha had that slightly detached feeling she often had when she was around them — as if she wasn't quite there. She felt like a spectator, not a participant. She had a textbook with her and tried to study despite the noise. It was hard to concentrate. It really wasn't the noise that was distracting her. It was that "out of it" feeling that made it hard to pay attention to what she was doing.

Little three-year-old Saraleh wandered into the room. She went up to Zahava and grabbed her around the waist. "Where are you going?" she asked.

"To a party, cutie pie."

"Can I come, too?" She looked up at Zahava with big, round eyes.

Zahava turned around and knelt down. "I don't think so, sweetie...."

Saraleh's eyes filled with tears.

"Don't cry, Saraleh." Zahava gave her a hug. "Tell you what — I'll ask Ima if you can ride in the car with us. Would you like that?" Saraleh nodded. "Come," said Zahava. "Let's go ask her now." They left the room to find Mrs. Baker.

"That was a good idea Zahava had," Dini said with approval.

"Yeah," agreed Rivka. "She's really good with Saraleh. She seems to understand her."

"Birds of a feather..." trilled Yochie.

"Yochie!"

"It really *was* a good idea..." Bracha began.

"Let's go, ladies!" Yochie urged. "It's party time!"

The quints threw her a hasty, "Bye, Bracha, see ya later," as they followed Yochie through the door at an eager clip.

"Why do I feel invisible sometimes?" Bracha asked the empty room. Abandoning her textbook, she stood up and began to wander around the house, looking for something to do.

Moishy was in his room, probably hatching some new scheme in that overactive mind of his. Chezky and Donny were out in the yard throwing a ball around. She was about to call to them to come in out of the rain when she noticed that the rain had stopped. It was still blustery and gray out, but it would take more than a couple of clouds and a few gusts of wind to keep Chezky inside.

She drifted into the baby's room. Rachel Ahuva was always so cute and fun to play with fresh from a nap. But the baby was still asleep in her crib.

"Rachel Ahuva?" she whispered. "Ruchie Ahuvie, babyleh?"

No answer. She covered the baby up and wandered over to the window. From this vantage point, she could see the Baker station wagon pulling out. Two of the quints were in the back, with Saraleh wedged between. They were laughing about something. They looked like they were having fun. And they weren't even at the party yet!

The house felt very quiet. Bracha's breath fogged up the window. Slowly and carefully she wrote "Bracha Baker," in English and in Hebrew. She stepped away and watched the words fade as the mist evaporated.

I wonder what time Abba's coming home tonight? she thought. *I wonder if it's a "home" Shabbos for Ashi?* She missed her big brother, away at yeshivah. *I hope he's coming and that he'll have time to talk.*

She rested her head in her hands. Then she laughed, a quiet mirthless laugh.

How is it, she thought, *that in a family of twelve children and two adults, I can feel so alone?*

3

Good News Times Three

The screen door banged open and Bracha burst into the kitchen. She was accompanied by a blast of frigid air.

"Ima! Guess what?" she shouted.

Mrs. Baker was at the stove, stirring something in a large pot. The kitchen was full of steam. It was a big old kitchen, the kind they used to call a farm kitchen. When they'd moved into the Wharton Mansion, their father had pointed out where the chimney used to be. Along one side of the room, above the ancient sinks, were two windows with wooden frames looking out onto the backyard. All of the cupboards were made of thick wood; no modern formica in this place. A door in one wall led to a large pantry, much to Mrs. Baker's delight. Because of this pantry she could now buy in bulk, a necessity in a large family. There was room for an extra freezer in there, too.

The Bakers' gleaming refrigerator and stove looked strangely out of place in this room. As for the microwave, it looked downright uncomfortable perched on the ancient counter.

"Hi, Bracha." Mrs. Baker turned her head to greet her daughter. Her cheeks were flushed nearly as red from the kitchen's heat as Bracha's were from the cold — and something else. "What's up?"

"Oh, Ima, I can hardly believe it!" Bracha looked about ready to explode. "I got the lead part in the school play!"

Mrs. Baker turned down the flame and reached for Bracha to hug her warmly. "Good for you, Bracha!" she exclaimed.

"It's a play based on the book *Legacy of Gold*," Bracha burst out, bubbling with excitement. "I'm so glad I read it last year! I'm going to be Moses Lazar. I was so nervous. Everyone wanted that part, it's really the best part.... I was so sure I'd mess up the reading but, *baruch Hashem*, it really went well. Everyone really read well. I don't know how Mrs. Portnoy could decide! *I* couldn't...but she did!"

Mrs. Baker nodded, smiling. "It's not an easy thing to do, giving out parts in a play."

"We only have a few weeks," Bracha continued breathlessly. "Ima, I have so many lines to memorize! And rehearsals! We'll have a couple of them a week, and the last week we'll have one every day! And we each have to come up with our own costume. I'm lucky that I have brothers — there's sure to be a beard in one of the Purim boxes...." She did a joyous skipping dance between the fridge and the table. "Oh, Ima, I can't believe it. I'm so excited!"

Her dance halted at the stove. "What's for supper?" she demanded, peering into the pot. "Noodles? How boring! I want to celebrate. What can we do to make them fancier?"

"Well, we could make a casserole," her mother offered, smiling fondly at her daughter.

"Good!" Bracha nodded happily. "I'll grate the cheese." She took out a dairy bowl and the grater and put them on the counter. She felt like she needed to do something with her hands, something practical. Otherwise she might float up into the air through sheer happiness! Who cared how many lines she had to memorize, or how hard she'd have to rehearse? One vision stood out in her mind, brighter than all the rest. Bracha Baker in the spotlight — at last!

As she went to the refrigerator to get the cheese, still lost in her visions, her brother Moishy burst through the door.

"Moishy, guess what?" she cried. "Your big sister got the lead part in the school play!"

"Wow, Bracha! Mazel tov! That's really great." Before Bracha could fill him in on the details, Moishy spun around. "Ima, guess what?"

"What is it, Moishy?"

"The rebbe announced today that every month there will be an award for the Most Valuable *Bochur* in our class. He's calling it the 'M.V.B.' award, for short. And there will be a prize! The winner will get to go to a *siyum haShas* that the rebbe will be making. And guess who'll be there? His Rosh Yeshivah! Isn't that great? The M.V.B. will get to meet the Rosh Yeshivah, in person!" Moishy rocked back on his heels, and then rose up on his toes as he rushed on. "I guess anyone could win it. We have a pretty good class.... It helps to have brains. I mean, if someone is one of the better students there's really a pretty good chance that he could get it if he tried. I mean, if someone is a good student anyway and gets good marks, then winning the M.V.B. award shouldn't be all that hard — if you know what I mean."

"And we definitely do know what — or should I say, *who* — you mean," Bracha said.

Moishy blushed. Bracha felt a twinge of remorse. After all, if her brother felt confident, it wasn't nice of her to burst his bubble. She tried to make it up to him.

"Anyway, Moish," she added warmly. "We have a lot of confidence in you. I'm sure you'll win."

"Thanks a lot." Moishy came to stand beside his sister. "What are you doing there?"

"Grating cheese for a casserole."

"What else is going in?"

"Just noodles so far."

"Hmmmm. It will need more than noodles and cheese. How about tuna fish? Ima, can I add some tuna to the casserole?"

"I don't see why not," said Mrs. Baker. "Go ahead."

Moishy went for the tuna and the can opener. As he opened the can he looked out the window. "Here come the quints," he announced.

"Zahava and Rivka tried out for parts and didn't get them," Bracha told her mother quietly.

"Wow, they must be disappointed," said Moishy.

The quints came into the kitchen, talking all at once.

"Why are you standing around in your coats?" Zahava asked.

Moishy and Bracha looked at each other in surprise. It was true — in the excitement they'd forgotten to take off their coats.

"Bracha!" yelled Yochie. "Mazel tov!" She flourished an arm. "Ladies, I would like to present to you Bracha Baker, our up-and-coming star!"

Moishy poked his head above Bracha's shoulder. "Don't applaud, just throw money!" he hinted.

"Moishy!" Dini protested. "Stop it! Bracha certainly isn't doing this for money."

"I should hope not," Rivka said primly. She went up to her mother and kissed her. "Hello, Ima!"

Mrs. Baker smiled. "Well, it's nice to get one hello."

Immediately, the rest of the quints surrounded their mother and covered her with hugs and kisses.

"Help!" she laughed. "I'm drowning!"

"I didn't get a part and I am so disappointed," Zahava frowned, once the welcome was over.

"I didn't get one either," said Rivka. "But I might still be able to help out with the music."

"That would be nice," Mrs. Baker nodded.

"I guess so...."

"I don't understand why I didn't get a part. It's never happened before," Zahava continued in a puzzled tone.

"Well, if you didn't flounce around the stage so much..." Dini began.

"What flounce? Who flounces?" Zahava retorted. "You can't just say the lines, you have to act a little. You have to be dramatic."

"I'm sure you were good," Tikva said soothingly. "*Legacy of Gold* is different from anything the school has done before. Maybe they were looking for a different style."

"That's right," Yochie chimed in. "Besides, they have to give other girls a chance." She turned to her younger brother, peering over his shoulder. "Moishy, what are you doing?"

"I'm adding tuna to the casserole."

"You're getting some on your coat." She leaned closer to sniff. "Yum! Ima, do you know what one friend of mine's mother always does? She puts in potato chips. Can I add potato chips?"

"Sounds interesting. Let's try it."

"Goody!" Yochie went to the pantry, followed by Rivka.

"Look," Rivka pointed. "Here's a can of string beans. They taste so good with melted cheese."

"Bring them along. Why not?"

They went back to the kitchen, to find everyone standing around the bowl where Bracha was mixing ingredients.

"Ketchup — it needs ketchup!" Zahava called.

"Anything with cheese definitely need garlic," Dini decided.

"Mustard powder," suggested Tikva.

"What?"

"Mustard powder gives it a really interesting flavor."

"Okay." Bracha smiled agreeably and sprinkled some in.

"Whoa!" said Mrs. Baker. "Hold your horses!" She moved to the center of the group, put a finger into the mixture, made a *berachah*, and licked. "It's just right, though I don't know how. Let's get this 'Baker Special' into the oven before something happens to it."

She poured the whole thing into a large pyrex dish. Before she could put it in the oven, the door was flung open again.

"Hello, all!"

"Abba!" The children clustered around their father.

"Oooh, you're cold," Zahava giggled.

"You're early!" said Rivka.

Bracha crowded up closer to her father. "Abba, guess what?"

Mr. Baker's face glowed with something more than just the wind. He looked excited. "It'll have to wait a minute, Bracha. I have some big news." He looked around. "Is everyone here?"

"Almost," Yochie said eagerly. "I'll get the other kids." She ran out of the room.

"What's the news, Abba?" asked Dini.

"Patience, my dear, I want everyone to hear." Mr. Baker looked around the room. "Why are all of you standing around in your coats?"

Yochie was soon back with Chezky, Donny, Saraleh, and even a sleepy Rachel Ahuva, whom she had woken from her nap.

"Oh, Yochie, you woke the baby!" Dini exclaimed.

"It's okay," said Mrs. Baker, taking the baby from Yochie. "I wanted her to wake up soon anyway."

"I hope this is important," Chezky declared. "Donny and I were busy."

"Me, too," said Saraleh. "With blocks!"

Mr. Baker picked up Saraleh, tossed her squealing in the air, and set her back down with a hug.

"Nu, Abba, what's the big news?" Moishy asked impatiently.

"Don't 'nu' your Abba, Moishy," said his mother.

"Well," said Mr. Baker, "here's the big news. As you may have heard, our local councilman had to retire and there's going to be a special election in four weeks."

"Yeah, we learned about that yesterday in current events," Dini said.

"Did we? I don't remember," said Zahava.

"Maybe if you paid more attention...."

"Quiet, kids," Mrs. Baker cut in. "Abba's trying to continue."

"Well," Mr. Baker announced, "guess who the party has asked to run for the council?"

"Who?"

"Me!"

"*You*?"

"Oh, Abba, that's fantastic!"

"Ephraim, really?" cried Mrs. Baker. "Oh, I'm so excited!"

"Wow, that's so neat!"

"Politics!" said Moishy in amazement. "I can't believe my father is going into politics!"

"Will there be a campaign?"

"Can we help?"

"Let's get buttons and bumper stickers: 'Vote for Baker!' "

"I'll vote for you, Abba," Chezky assured his father.

Mr. Baker laughed. "I'm afraid you have to be over eighteen to vote, Chezky."

"That means that only Ima can vote for you. Not even Ashi is big enough." Tikva was disappointed.

"It's just as well," Yochie shrugged. "If all of us could vote, Abba would win by a landslide. This way the other candidates will have a chance."

Everyone laughed. Bracha saw her chance.

"That's such good news, Abba. I have some good news, too...."

Before she could get out the words, Mr. Baker spotted the casserole.

"One second, Bracha. What's that?" he asked, pointing to the colorful mixture.

Mrs. Baker gave a slightly apologetic smile. "Dinner," she said. "A group effort."

"Looks interesting." He snapped his fingers. "Hey, I have an idea. We ought to celebrate tonight. Let's stick this tribute to teamwork in the fridge and go out to eat!"

"Yay!"

"The vote's unanimous!" shouted Moishy. "It's a good thing we kept on our coats!" He led the rush to the car.

Soon the kitchen was empty except for Bracha and her parents. Mrs. Baker handed the baby to her husband and started wrapping up the casserole.

"Abba?"

"Yes, Bracha?"

"Abba, I got the lead role in the school play."

"Good for you! That's wonderful! I'm very proud of you."

Outside, the car horn hooted. Mr. Baker smiled absentmindedly at Bracha and went out the door, bearing Rachel Ahuva. Mrs. Baker rushed past with her bag of bottles and diapers. "Lock up, Bracha, will you?"

Bracha turned off the kitchen light. For some reason, she wasn't as excited as she'd been before. Running for town council seemed so much more important than being in a play. Somehow, the spotlight seemed to have shifted....

The horn hooted again, loud and long. Bracha sighed. There was no time to sort out all her confused feelings now. She locked the kitchen door and ran to join her family.

4

M.V.B. in Training

N ashim va'avadim u'ketanim, peturim min ha-sukkah....' "

Chezky sat up in bed and squinted at the clock on the wall. "Moishy! What time is it?" Sleepily, he tried to focus on his brother, sitting at the desk in his pajamas. "Moishy, what are you doing?"

"It's a quarter to seven. 'Katan she'aino tzarich le'emo, chayav basukkah,' " Moishy droned on in a sing-song voice. "Go back to sleep."

"Have you completely and totally lost your mind?" Chezky demanded. He got out of bed and walked unsteadily over to the desk. "You're memorizing *mishnayos*? *Now*?"

" '*Maaseh...*' " Moishy stopped in mid-note. "It bothers you?"

"Who, me? No, why should it bother me?" Chezky shrugged his shoulders and pointed to himself. "If you want to get up before dawn and memorize *mishnayos*, who am I to say anything? After all, you're a guest here until they can get that leaky pipe in your room fixed!" He waved his arms and staggered back to his bed. "Just because everyone else in the entire world is asleep.... Who am I to say anything to an honored guest!"

"Go back to sleep, Chezky," Moishy advised. He turned calmly back to the desk. " '*Katan she'aino tzarich....*' Where was I?" He ran his finger down the page.

"*Maaseh,*" called Donny from under his quilt.

"You're awake, too?" Moishy glared at the lump under the quilt.

"Yes," answered Donny.

"Go back to sleep."

"There's really no reason to go back to sleep," Chezky told him. "We have to get up at seven, anyway."

"Well, go wash *negel vasser* or something." Moishy pointedly turned back to his *sefer*.

"Yes, sir, Mr. Masmid, sir!" Chezky saluted. "Come on, Donny, let's go together." They left the room.

Moishy stared down at the page. " '*Maaseh....* ' " he began. "Aach! It's no good. My concentration has been ruined — utterly decimated!" Despite his frustration he took a moment to enjoy his own words. "Decimated!"

he said again. What a great word. With a sigh, he closed his Mishnah and began to dress.

At breakfast, Mrs. Baker commented on his new morning routine. "I hear you've turned into an early bird, Moishy."

"I really want to take this M.V.B. award seriously," Moishy replied. "I think I have a good chance. It would be so exciting to win and get to meet my rebbe's Rosh Yeshivah." He shrugged. "Anyway, I'm trying."

"Well, good for you, Moishy," Mrs. Baker smiled. "We're all cheering for you. But you won't lose too much sleep over this, will you?"

"Don't worry, Ima, I won't." He grinned. "I don't want to be too tired to go to the *siyum*."

The boys usually enjoyed walking to school together. Sometimes they would make it into an adventure, pretending to be great explorers, or prisoners escaping from some unseen enemy. Sometimes the game would be relevant to the season: around Chanukah time they would pretend they were going to a secret yeshivah, in defiance of the Greek decrees. Before Purim they'd be the school children that Mordechai met. Before Pesach they'd cross the Red Sea.

Other times they would just talk — or rather, Moishy would talk and the others would listen. Moishy almost always had something interesting to say. Today, though, was a little different. Moishy muttered *mishnayos* to himself all the way to school. Chezky and Donny walked beside him, maintaining a respectful silence.

Muttering an absentminded farewell to his brothers, Moishy separated from them and went up to his classroom. He used the minutes after he'd finished *Shemonah Esrei*, while waiting for the others to finish, to quietly recite *mishnayos* to himself. Everyone put their siddurim away, but the rebbe didn't tell them to take out their books. *What's up?* wondered Moishy.

"I have an announcement to make," the rebbe began. Was it about the M.V.B. award? thought Moishy, in rising excitement.

"From today on," the rebbe continued, "we will be spending one hour a day learning with a *chavrusah*. Each student will be assigned a partner...."

Moishy didn't listen any more. *Chavrusah* learning! He'd been waiting for this for years! You could really learn a lot with a *chavrusah*. *If I get to learn with the right guy*, he thought, we can go really far. *This will really help with the M.V.B.!*

The rebbe went on speaking. He discussed the advantages of learning *bechavrusah* and how to go about it. Moishy hardly heard him; his mind was racing ahead. He could just see it now: Moshe Baker, *talmid chacham* and wonder child of yeshivah! He hardly noticed when the rebbe started assigning partners — until he heard his name called.

"Moshe Baker will learn with Berel Oberlander."

Berel Oberlander? Berel Oberlander? Oh no! Moishy's dream shattered into a million pieces. *There must be some mistake! How can I learn with Berel Oberlander?*

He's so slow! He'll hold me back. I'll go out of my mind! I can't learn with Berel Oberlander. I'll never get the award! What am I going to do? Berel Oberlander! I'll speak to the rebbe during recess. He won't make me learn with Berel Oberlander....

Recess had never seemed so long in coming. Finally, when the bell rang, he leapt out of his seat and ran up to the front desk.

"Rebbe," he said. "Rebbe, may I speak with you for a minute?"

The rebbe with the bushy brown beard glanced up at the boy, smiling. "Certainly, Moishy, what can I do for you?"

Now that he was actually confronted with the problem of explaining to the rebbe why he didn't want to learn with Berel Oberlander, Moishy found himself a little tongue-tied.

"Well, um, it's like this.... Berel is a good guy and all, and a *masmid*, too. It would be good to learn with him, but — well, he doesn't *chap* very fast. Know what I mean? It takes him longer to catch on than it takes me. I'm worried I'll get, uh, well, kind of bored if I learn with him. I mean, waiting for him to figure things out..."

The rebbe looked at him steadily. "Yes, I hear what you're saying."

Moishy continued, heartened. "So I would like to ask the rebbe to change my *chavrusah*." He waited hopefully.

"No, Moishy, I'm not going to change your *chavrusah*." The rebbe sounded decided.

Moishy's face fell.

"I put a lot of thought into setting up these learning teams," Rabbi Weinreb continued, "and I feel this is the best setup for both of you." He leaned back in his chair. "Berel isn't exactly dumb, you know."

Moishy was horrified. "I didn't mean to say..." he stammered.

"I know you didn't, but that's the way it came out, didn't it? If you look at the record, his marks are about as high, on the average, as your own. And he knows how to apply himself." He looked at Moishy meaningfully. "So now that you have the *chavrusah*, what are you going to do about your problem?"

Moishy gulped. "I don't know.... Uh, I guess if I have some spare time while Berel is thinking, I could always memorize some more *mishnayos*." He brightened. "Memorizing *mishnayos* isn't too hard for me. I've already done 137!" He looked at the rebbe for approval.

The rebbe smiled at him. "Okay, Moishy," he said. "You give it a try." He stood up and touched his student on the shoulder. "If you have any more problems, please bring them to me."

"Sure, Rebbe. Thank you."

"You're welcome, Moishy. Good luck with your learning." The rebbe left the room.

Moishy learned with Berel for the first time that afternoon. It didn't go too badly. There were even a few times when he felt that he'd helped Berel understand a difficult point. He spoke to Chezky about it on the way home.

"So you see, Chezky, I can really help this kid out. I'm pretty sure that's why the rebbe put me with him. I guess he figured that I wouldn't be held back, since I can learn so fast." At this point Moishy began to wonder if it sounded like he was boasting. "Anyway," he finished quickly, "I don't think it will hurt my chances for the M.V.B. award."

"Probably not," agreed Chezky. "Wow, now you're a rebbe too."

"Well, not exactly...."

"Close enough. I'll never get even that far!" He gave Moishy an affectionate punch in the arm. "Well, chalk up another one for the Baker genius!"

Moishy blushed, and ducked his head. "C'mon," he urged, to cover up his embarrassment. "Race you home!"

At dinner, the place at the head of the table was noticeably empty.

"Where's Abba?" Moishy asked Bracha.

"Where have you been? He had to stay late to work on the campaign."

"He'll probably be having a lot of late nights from now on," Rivka put in. "That's politics for you."

"Oh." Moishy stared at his father's empty place. Wasn't their move to the Wharton Mansion supposed to mean that Abba would spend more time with the family? He'd wanted to tell him about their new learning *chavrusos*. Dinner time was when Abba caught up on the family's news.

Well, I guess I'll see him on Shabbos, Moishy thought. Shabbos seemed a long way off.

He sighed. What Abba was doing was great — but dinner without him was just no fun!

5

The Play's the Thing

L adies, please put your pencils down and pass your papers forward."

Bracha breathed a big sigh of relief. *I hate surprise quizzes,* she thought. *But I don't think I did too badly.... Though I'm not so sure about problem four....*

"Psst! Pass up the quiz!" Her friend Esty was tapping on her shoulder from the seat behind.

Bracha reached back to get the paper offered her. She was about to pass it on when Esty kicked her seat. This made her look down at what she was holding in her hand. It wasn't a quiz! Leave it to Esty to figure out a new way to pass notes. She put the page on her lap and read:

Dear Bracha,
That wasn't so bad, was it? I'm not sure about problem four. Or seven.
Why are you yawning your head off? Did you stay up all night studying?
Don't forget we have play rehearsal today. Are you nervous? I am! I still can't believe that Yehudis got that part! Do you know all of your lines yet?
Don't write back — too risky!

Love, Esty

Bracha laughed quietly to herself. *That's my friend Esty! I didn't realize I was yawning so much. Maybe it wasn't such a good idea to stay up so late memorizing my lines. Today is only the first rehearsal — there's still plenty of time to get my part down perfectly. Oh well, too late now.*

She glanced at her watch. Five minutes until the bell! She looked around the room. Only four girls in her class were in the play: Esty, Yehudis, Gitty Miller, and herself. She glanced over at Yehudis, who was looking at her watch, too. *I'll bet she's more nervous than I am! After tryouts all anyone could talk about was the surprise choice of Yehudis to play Matthews. A lot of people were saying she got picked because she was new at school.* Bracha frowned. She wished she'd paid more attention to Yehudis's tryout.... Well, that was *lashon hara* — whether it was true or not. Or *rechilus*, or something.... Anyway, she didn't think Mrs. Portnoy would do that. Bracha looked around guiltily, as if people could read her thoughts.

The bell rang. Bracha jumped up and began to pack her school bag. Esty came up to her, grinning broadly.

"Aren't you going to answer any of my questions?"

"Esty," Bracha shook her finger at her friend. "One of these days you're going to get us in a lot of trouble!"

"Probably!" Esty winked.

The girls said good-bye to their teacher and left the classroom. Right outside the door Bracha stopped and took out the note. She held it in front of her and tilted her head as if reading.

"Dear Esty," she said. "No, the quiz was not so bad. I also don't know about problem four. I'm 'yawning my head off' because I am tired. I *was* up late — not studying math, studying my lines. I didn't forget about rehearsal. No comment on the next part.... No, I don't know all of my lines yet, but I'm getting there. I wouldn't dream of writing back — living dangerously is not my thing! Love, Bracha."

Esty giggled. "Should I write back, or should we just talk?"

"Talk, please! I'll get writer's cramp!" The girls laughed together.

"I'm glad someone's laughing," eighth-grader Gitty Miller came up behind them. "Are you going to rehearsal? I can't believe how they divided up the parts! I don't mean you, Bracha, you deserved that part. But why'd they give that big part to Yehudis? My sister said that she didn't even know Yehudis could talk, she's so quiet!"

Bracha looked nervously over at Esty. This was *lashon hara* — no question about it. How could she get out of this? Quickly, she looked at her watch. "Help!" she cried. "We're late! Let's run!" Without waiting for a reply she turned and ran down the hall, the other girls hurrying after her.

They came to a breathless stop, sliding through the doors of the auditorium in a grand pileup. Every head turned to see what the commotion was all about.

"What's up?" someone shouted.

Bracha tried to be nonchalant. "We just thought we were late, that's all." She threw herself into a seat with an exaggerated "Whew!" *Double whew!* she thought to herself.

Bracha loved the auditorium of the Bais Yaakov of Bloomfield. It was new, like the whole building. Big and long, it was filled with seats that sloped down to the stage. The chairs had arms and fold-up seats. The first three rows were padded. The vast room was painted a warm blue with mauve accents. But it was the stage that held Bracha's attention.

The stage was enormous, and had everything you would need to put on a play: good lighting, a striped double curtain, and even dressing rooms! A small row of steps led up to the stage on either side. There was a separate entrance behind, where Bracha and her fellow actresses would wait for their cues to step out in front of the audience....

"Ladies!" Mrs. Portnoy, the social studies teacher who doubled as director of school productions, clapped her hands to call her cast to order. Bracha was jolted out of her reverie. "Come, ladies, let's get moving! Will everyone come down to the front, please!"

Bracha picked up her things and moved along the aisle toward the front of the auditorium, looking for a place to sit. She spotted one seat three rows back, and another right before the stage, next to Yehudis.

She glanced around. Esty was sitting comfortably between two other girls. *I guess she won't mind if I sit up here*, Bracha thought. *I might as well be friendly; we're going to be working together a lot.* She walked quickly down the aisle and slid into the seat next to Yehudis.

"Hi." Yehudis gave a shy grin.

"Hi," said Bracha with an answering smile.

"Ladies, a little quiet, please!" Mrs. Portnoy stood just below the stage, facing them. "Thank you all for coming and for being on time. I assume that everyone has been able to get a copy of the book and has aquired a feeling for the story. After much discussion it has been decided to dispense with Australian and English accents."

Some of the girls groaned in disappointment. Bracha was relieved; her English accent sounded a bit strange, at least to her ears.

"Today we're going to walk through our parts and get clear the staging: exits and entrances, who goes where when, and so on. I hope everyone has her script. Please remember, the sooner you memorize your lines the smoother things will go."

I'm glad I started already, Bracha thought. She was tempted to do the first scene without a script. No, she decided, it might look like she was showing off.

"Okay, ladies. We're ready to begin." Mrs. Portnoy glanced at the first page of her playscript. "Let's have 'Moses Lazar' and the judge up on the stage, please."

A thrill ran down Bracha's spine. This was it! With Yehudis behind her, she climbed up the stage steps and took her place onstage. Yehudis waited in the wings for her scene.

Esty played the judge who would sentence poor Moses Lazar to jail in Australia. Bracha approved of the choice. Esty was a good actress but didn't have the patience to do a lot of memorizing. Although the judge was important to the story, the part itself was pretty short.

The first scene went smoothly. Even though it was just a walk-through, Esty played her part well. She had described her costume to Bracha before rehearsal; she'd managed to get hold of a white wig and black gown. Bracha began to feel really excited. This was going to be good!

The next scene, set on the boat, took a while to figure out. There were a lot of people in it and much discussion on how to arrange the set to make the whole thing look more boatlike.

In the following scene Moses Lazar met his employer-to-be, Matthews. This was Yehudis's first time on the stage. She walked briskly to the center, a tall girl with shoulder-length hair and calm gray eyes. *I wonder if she's nervous*, thought Bracha. *She doesn't look it. Good for her!*

"Okay, ladies, from the top!" Mrs. Portnoy called. "Bracha on the left. Yehudis, approach from the right."

Yehudis/Matthews glanced at her script and strode forward. "What are you carrying there, man?"

"I'm a Jew. I pray with these," answered Bracha/Lazar.

"Can you be trusted, Jew?"

"To trust you?"

Yehudis chuckled. "I like a humorous fellow...."

"Maybe stand a little closer, Yehudis," suggested Mrs. Portnoy.

As the rehearsal went on, Bracha liked what she saw more and more. Yehudis was good. She could project her voice, and she listened to instructions. She seemed really confident. Even though this was a first reading she was putting some feeling into her lines. She was a fine actress who certainly deserved her part. So much for *lashon hara*!

Mrs. Portnoy looked at the big clock in the back of the auditorium. "Oy, it's late!" She clapped her hands for attention. "We'll finish up here and continue next time — on Wednesday." She rolled up her script. "You're doing a lovely job and I'm sure we'll have a wonderful play. Right, ladies, I'll see you in a few days." She tucked the script into her handbag and beamed at the actresses.

"Yehudis, wait for me," said Bracha as they climbed off the stage. "We can walk together."

Esty and the other girls joined them. They walked home slowly, discussing the play from every angle.

"Bracha, you sure make a terrific Moses," Esty complimented.

Bracha glowed. "Thanks, Judge. You're not so bad yourself." She turned to Yehudis. "You were really professional, Yehudis."

"Yeah," Esty agreed warmly. "You're a really good actress."

Bracha persisted, "Did you feel as confident as you looked up there?"

Yehudis blushed. "Well, you guys did say I'm a good actress...."

The others laughed with her. They continued on their way. One by one, the girls said good-bye as they reached their homes or intersections. Finally there were just Bracha and Yehudis.

"Where do you live?" Bracha asked. "I thought we were the farthest from the school."

"On Redwood. The house on the corner," Yehudis replied. "One block farther than you."

The girls walked quietly for a while. As they neared the Baker residence, Yehudis exclaimed, "I love your house!"

"Really?"

"It's so beautiful and old-fashioned! I love old houses. It must be such fun to live in."

"When we first moved in I didn't like it so much," Bracha confessed. "It's a little run-down. We thought it was haunted. There were all sorts of weird noises and stuff. Some of them turned out to be my brothers and sisters playing tricks. They thought it was funny. I didn't!" Bracha made a face. "Then my brother Chezky and two of my sisters found an old tunnel under the house. It used to be part of the 'Underground Railroad' when there were slaves. The tunnel was being used by counterfeiters! The police caught them. Boy, was that ever scary!"

Yehudis was listening, enthralled. "Wow, I'll bet it was!"

"Hmmm!" Bracha agreed with an emphatic nod. She looked up at the old house. "Now I guess I like it. I don't really think about it anymore. It's home." A thought occurred to her. "You just moved, too. How do you like your new house?"

"It's nice. Bigger than the apartment in New York that we used to live in." She looked straight at Bracha. "Would you like to come over some time?"

"Sure. I really would. Anyway, we ought to rehearse together. There's a lot of stuff to go over." Bracha's face lit up with a sudden idea. "Let's have a couple of sleep-overs! We could take it in turns, once by you, once by me." Bracha stopped as she realized she might be imposing. "That is, if you think it would be okay with your mother."

Yehudis's eyes sparkled. "I'm pretty sure it would be okay, as long as we didn't stay up too late. I'll just have to check out which nights are good." She smiled at Bracha.

"Good," said Bracha. "Give me your phone number so we can be in touch."

"You'd better take mine, too."

Yehudis got a pad and pen from her bag. The girls exchanged numbers. There was an awkward pause as they tried to figure out a graceful way to say good-bye. Suddenly Yehudis grinned.

"Good-bye, 'Lazar,' " she said, holding out her hand.

Bracha grasped her hand and shook it. "Goodbye, 'Matthews'!"

As Bracha walked up the drive to her house she thought about Yehudis. *It must be hard to move to another town. Maybe Yehudis was so quiet because she was feeling out of things. She really is a nice person; I like her.*

Her first play rehearsal — and the beginning of a nice new friendship! All in all, it had been a pretty good day.... She ran into the house, banging the back door behind her. She found her mother in the kitchen.

"Hello, Ima darling!" She flung her arms around her mother.

"Well, well, well," said Mrs. Baker, responding in kind. "What did I do to deserve this?"

"Just being you!" Bracha released her mother and opened the refrigerator. "What's for snack?"

"Fruit."

Bracha made a face and took an apple.

"How did rehearsal go?" Mrs. Baker asked, reaching past her daughter to take some cucumbers and tomatoes from the vegetable bin.

"Really well," Bracha told her. "Remember that new girl I told you about — Yehudis Klein, the one who was picked for Matthews? Let me tell you, she is one good actress! It's really going to be a pleasure working with her."

"I'm glad to hear that," Mrs. Baker said, beginning to prepare a salad.

"And she's a super person, too. I think I found myself a new friend." Bracha twisted her apple core around by the stem.

"That's really nice," her mother smiled. "It's good to have friends. And it's very nice for her, too. It's not easy being a new girl in school."

"Yes," agreed Bracha. "Anyway, we'll have to work together a lot. I thought it would be a good idea to rehearse together, just me and her. We thought we'd have a couple of sleep-overs — if it's all right with you, that is. And with her mother."

"I don't see why not, as long as it isn't every night."

"I don't think it will be every night, Ima." Bracha gave her mother a sidelong glance.

"Only every other night," Mrs. Baker returned with a straight face.

Bracha laughed. "Oh, Ima, I love you!" She jumped up and gave her mother a kiss. "I've got homework to do. See ya later." She flew out of the kitchen. Mrs. Baker watched her go with a smile on her lips. It was good to see her daughter so happy.

Bracha and Yehudis spent a lot of time together over the next week. Most of the time they went to Yehudis's house, where they could have peace and quiet. Yehudis had only two brothers, one who was much older than her and one much younger. Her mother worked full-time and very often Yehudis was alone.

"It's so quiet here," Bracha said on the first day they met there. "So peaceful."

"I guess so," Yehudis said. "But sometimes I get lonely. I wish I had a sister, preferably one near my age."

"Well, I've got seven, and it's not as easy as it looks!"

"Yes, but your house always seems so full, and so busy and fun...."

"That's not so surprising — seeing as we have only fourteen people living there!" The girls laughed together.

Then Yehudis stopped laughing. "Still, I wouldn't mind getting to know your family — all of them," she said wistfully.

Bracha nodded sympathetically. Secretly, though, she had other plans. She had no desire to get Yehudis involved in all the hustle and bustle that went on in the Baker household. Maybe she'd feel differently later on...but for right now, she wanted to keep her new friend all to herself.

6
Tikva's Diary #1

Dear Diary,

I guess I should start off by introducing myself. My name is Tikva Baker. I am almost five feet tall. I have light brown hair, long and straight; brown eyes; glasses; and braces.

I have eleven brothers and sisters. Four of my sisters and I are quintuplets. When we were born, all the newspapers around these parts made a big deal about the five of us. I guess being a quint is something pretty special. It's unusual, anyway. Except for that, I feel just like anybody else.

My father is an attorney, my mother an artist. We live in Bloomfield, in a big old mansion that was built sometime before the Civil War. It's got a huge front and backyard, including some woods and even a pond, that go with the house. I loved our old house, too, but I have to admit it's great to have all this space.

Oh, one other thing. I am legally blind. There was a problem with oxygen deprivation when I was born, which left me blind in one eye and nearly blind in the other. I wear very thick glasses, and can tell the difference between light and dark, and see very big shapes. At night I can't see anything.

I've decided to keep this diary for several reasons. First of all, I'd like to remember things that happen to me and my family. Second of all, I'd like to write about how I feel and what I think. My older sister, Bracha, has a diary and says that when she's upset, she writes in her diary and it helps calm her down.

I could use some calming these days — but more on that later....

Because of my sight problem, what I write here can't be really private because I can't read the printout. I'll print it out anyway, to preserve it. I could always have Yochie read it. If you're wondering how I can write it, I know how to touch-type. In case it isn't obvious, I'm using a computer. Maybe someday I'll be able to read it myself. Who knows? There's always hope. (Tikva means hope. I have to live up to my name!)

Now I'll tell you why I'm so upset.

Actually, things didn't start off so badly. My father is running for the town council. Today our living room turned into a campaign headquarters. We were *all stuffing envelopes with flyers. We set up a sort of assembly line. My job was to seal the envelopes and to put them in neat piles in a box. Actually, it was fun. Yochie made up this really funny song called "Stuffing Envelopes for Abba" and we were all in hysterics!*

Saraleh came in to see what was so funny. She "helped" us, too — mostly by spilling so many flyers on the floor that it looked like we had a paper carpet! Things were going pretty smoothly, until my older sister Bracha walked in.

She was with her new friend, Yehudis, who is starring with her in the school play. I don't really know how it happened, but the next thing I knew, Yehudis was stuffing envelopes with us. She really got into it, moving at lightning speed and laughing at all of the jokes, even Moishy's dumb puns. We didn't mind a bit, but Bracha sounded upset. I think they were supposed to rehearse or something.

After a while everyone began to get hungry. Since I was taking a break just then, Rivka asked me to go to the pantry to get some potato chips. Yehudis jumped up and said that if we would tell her where the pantry was, she'd get them. You could tell from her voice that she was wondering how in the world I could find potato chips in a pantry. Some people don't seem to understand that blind doesn't equal helpless!

I was stuck for what to say but Yochie just told her: "No, thanks, Yehudis, you're busy. Tikva will take care of it." Good old Yochie! I left the room as fast as I could.

While I was in the kitchen, Moishy came home. He was feeling pretty low. It seems he messed up on some homework questions on the parashah. He'd forgotten all about it and had spent all of last night memorizing mishnayos instead. His rebbe was really upset with him. His rebbe said that he could make up the work, but Moishy needed help. I tried to help him but they were really hard questions.

So he came back to the living room to stuff envelopes. I was yelled at because the potato chips took so long coming. (I hope Yehudis didn't think I had trouble finding them.)

We stuffed for a while longer (there are a lot of flyers!) till Ima came in and asked how we were doing. I think we impressed her: we'd already done over a hundred. Then Moishy asked her when Abba was coming home. When Ima told him that Abba would be late because of political meetings and stuff, Moishy blew up! He told Ima that he really needed help with his homework and Abba was never home anymore, and we hadn't seen him at dinner for practically a week!

Yochie said: "Yeah!" and Rivka and Zahava and Dini and I agreed. We thought we'd be seeing more of Abba since the move to our new house — not less! Bracha didn't say anything, but Yochie told me later that you could see from the look on her face that she agreed, too.

Then Saraleh started crying: "I want Abba! I want Abba!" Yehudis, looking uncomfortable, said she was sorry to leave like this but her mother said she had to be home by five. Bracha walked her to the door and then clumped noisily up the stairs. Moishy said that if Bracha didn't have to stuff envelopes anymore, he didn't either. And he ran upstairs.

After we got Saraleh to stop crying, Ima said she thought we'd done enough for today, so we cleaned up and put everything in the study. I went upstairs to think about a new poem that had been forming in my mind.

When I passed Bracha's room I suddenly remembered that I'd left my CD player in her room and I thought I'd listen to some CDs. I went in without knocking (mistake!) and there was Bracha, crying on the bed! I asked if there was anything I could do to help and she said no, it was okay, and thank you, and would I please close the door behind me. I thought that this was very grown-up of her. A lot of people would have yelled at me for coming in without knocking.

Anyway, the mood in the house is gloomy. I wish my father had never started this campaign. At first we were excited, but now it looks like we'll hardly ever get to see Abba again, and everyone is so miserable.

Now I'll have to call Yochie to save this file.... No, I've changed my mind. I know which buttons to push, I'll do it myself. Though when I'll ever get to read it, who knows....

Love,
Tikva

7

A Real-Life Drama

Bracha was late to school on purpose, something she never did. She could think of only one other time she'd done such a thing: when she was in fourth grade and Ashi wrote on her face with indelible marker. Her mother had scrubbed and scrubbed but there were still a lot of marks left. Bracha had thought that if she could get to school during davening, people wouldn't have as much time to notice. So she'd pretended to have a stomachache.

It's funny how a person can feel guilty about these things years later, Bracha thought wryly. That time, Mrs. Baker had written a note for her teacher. This time, she decided to take her medicine instead. As she ran out of the house she felt her mother's eyes following her. *It was nice of Ima not to say anything,* Bracha thought. *I can feel her thinking that it's very unlike me to be late to school. I think I must be honest sometime about the last time I did this. And about this time, too — sometime. But now I just want to think!*

Bracha walked slowly, looking down. Her mind was blank. Occasionally she would kick some small rock or deliberately step on a crack. When she got to a crossing she would pull her head up, heavily, as if it were weighted down. Very often she would sigh.

It's not really surprising that I'm feeling so low, she thought. *I can't understand some of my sisters; how can they be so cheerful when so much is going wrong? Moishy's the only one who seems to realize what's going on, and he's no help. He's just acting really immature and impossible.*

She reviewed last night's scene. All of those horrible envelopes and flyers — the living room looked awful, like a paper tornado had hit the place. And that stupid song Yochie had made up!

But Yehudis hadn't thought it was awful. She'd liked it. She wanted to join them. Before Bracha had known what was happening, her costar — who should have been up in Bracha's room with her, rehearsing their lines for the play — was seated between Rivka and Yochie, stuffing envelopes like there was no tomorrow, and laughing heartily at every dumb joke.

It happens every time, Bracha thought bitterly. *Just when I think I've got a friend, she gets snatched away by my sisters. Everything they do becomes a sensation, just because there are five of them. I'm so boring in comparison. I feel like a nonentity!*

She was almost at school. How to face Yehudis, the way she was feeling? *I don't want it to happen again,* she thought defiantly. *It's just not fair. This time I can stop things before they go too far.*

Bracha lifted her head and picked up her pace. *I'm going to talk to Yehudis,* she decided. *I'm not going to let my family do me out of another good friend.*

As she approached the school building she began to feel nervous. She hated being late. *I really should have worked out my problems another time,* she thought. Lingering outside her classroom door, she screwed up her courage. Then, with a shrug, she went in to face the music.

Heads turned as she opened the door and slipped inside. Everyone stared. Tiptoeing to her seat, she felt her face grow hot.

"Good morning, Bracha," said the teacher. "We're glad you're here. Is everything okay?"

"Yes, Mrs. Levine," Bracha answered in a soft voice. "I'm sorry I'm late." She swallowed once. "I don't really have a good excuse."

There was a pause. Then Mrs. Levine smiled and said, "These things happen — though not to you so far, this year. I'm sure it won't happen again." She stood up and went to the blackboard.

Whew! *There certainly are some big advantages to having a good record,* Bracha thought in relief. *I was scared that I would have to stay after school or something. And today we have rehearsal!*

She looked over at Yehudis, who was absorbed in her Chumash. *I'll speak to her during lunch,* she decided. She opened her own Chumash and began to read.

Bracha davened during the midmorning break. It wasn't a very good davening, as she only had ten minutes. She really hated doing that. *Well,* she thought, *never again. It's not worth my while to work out my problems during time that's meant for other things.*

It wasn't hard to get Yehudis alone. The girls settled in a corner of the lunchroom and began eating with relish.

"We had my grandmother's chopped liver last night," Yehudis mumbled conversationally through a full mouth. "She came up from the city for Shabbos and brought us a big supply. I'm the only one in my family that likes it — besides my parents, I mean. I think it's great. I could have it every day."

"It's supposed to be good for you," Bracha remarked. "We had fish."

"Tuna?"

"No, fish sticks. I like to have them with ketchup and mayonnaise."

"Sounds good," said Yehudis agreeably. She hesitated, glancing at Bracha. "Why were you late this morning?"

"Oh, I don't know..." Bracha said vaguely.

"It must be something to see — your family getting out in the morning, I mean."

"I don't think it's any busier than any other big family."

"I wouldn't know," said Yehudis. "I only have two brothers. And no sisters."

"My mother has things pretty organized," said Bracha. She wiped her hands and opened her box of juice.

"I'll bet she has to be. Your mother is so neat! I don't know how she does it!"

"No one does," said Bracha. "My mother says that she's not even sure herself." She chuckled. "My Bubbie always looks at her and shakes her head and says, 'The *Aibishter* gives *ko'ach.*'"

"He sure does!" Yehudis agreed. The girls ate without talking for a while.

"Rehearsals are going well, don't you think so?" Yehudis asked finally.

"I guess so...."

"What do you mean you 'guess so'?"

"Well, I guess they're going well," said Bracha. "I just thought that we'd be further along by now."

Yehudis looked at her incredulously. "Are you serious?"

"Yes," Bracha looked down at the table and picked at a crumb. "We've wasted a little time, you know."

"When?" Yehudis was bewildered.

"Well, like yesterday. We were supposed to rehearse and you stuffed envelopes instead."

"That was hardly a waste of time..." began Yehudis.

"It's not as if they needed the help," Bracha interrupted. Now that she had begun, she wanted to get it all off her chest. "And you came over to my house especially to rehearse."

"But Bracha, I don't think stuffing envelopes for your father's campaign is a waste of time. It was helping your father. *And* it was fun! Your family makes everything seem fun."

"I guess it is more fun hanging out with my sisters than with me," Bracha said stiffly. "But we happen to have a play to put on."

"For goodness sake," Yehudis was on the defensive. "One hour isn't going to make it or break it."

"One thing can lead to another," Bracha said ominously.

"You act like I don't care about the play."

"Well, do you?"

"Of course I do!" Yehudis replied indignantly. "But I don't have to live it morning, noon, and night."

"I never said you did," said Bracha. "Just don't let my family get in our way."

Yehudis could only stare at Bracha. She couldn't believe her ears. Bracha realized she may have gone too far. Awkwardly she began, "I just want the play to go smoothly...." The bell rang.

"I see..." said Yehudis. It was clear that she didn't. She looked puzzled and angry. She stood up and began to gather up the debris from their lunch, muttering, "We'd better get back."

With rapid steps she crossed to the trash can to throw away the wrappings and crusts, and left the lunchroom. Bracha followed her out.

Bracha felt vaguely uncomfortable all afternoon. The conversation with Yehudis hadn't gone the way she'd pictured it. She had hoped to explain how lonely and insignificant she sometimes felt beside the quints, and why she'd been upset with Yehudis for stuffing envelopes instead of rehearsing with her. She had been so sure Yehudis would understand. *I guess it's hard for her to relate to my problem, seeing as she has only two brothers*, she thought to herself. *But you'd think that she'd at least try.*

It didn't occur to Bracha that she may not have done a very good job of explaining things to her friend. She'd sort of expected Yehudis to read her mind....

When the last bell rang she looked around for Yehudis. They usually went down to the auditorium together for play rehearsals. But Yehudis had already left on her own. Only Esty was waiting in the almost empty classroom.

"Where's Yehudis?" Bracha asked Esty.

"I don't know," Esty replied. "She was here a minute ago. Maybe she had something to do before rehearsal."

"Maybe," Bracha agreed. She finished packing her bookbag. "Come on, let's go." The two girls left the classroom.

When they got to the auditorium, Mrs. Portnoy was already there. Yehudis was sitting in the front row, looking at her script. Bracha hurried down the aisle and put her bookbag on the next seat. "Yehudis, I —"

"Bracha! Yehudis! On stage!" Mrs. Portnoy clapped her hands briskly. "We're starting where we left off yesterday, the scene where Matthews tells Lazar that he's sending for his family. Come now, let's begin."

Yehudis and Bracha climbed onto the stage. An old desk and chair stood at the center; the real scenery would be made later. Yehudis, as Matthews, sat behind the desk. Bracha, as Lazar, waited in the wings.

Yehudis picked up some papers, pretending to be absorbed in them. She made a few marks with a pencil and hummed to herself. Then she put the papers down and strolled over to where the window would be when the scenery was made.

"Who's that there?" she shouted out the "window." "Darcy! Darcy. Find Lazar and send him to me!" She looked out the "window" for a while as if checking to see if Darcy was doing his bidding. Then, satisfied, she sat down at the desk and resumed her writing and humming.

"Very good, Yehudis," called Mrs. Portnoy.

Yehudis dropped character for a moment to grin at the teacher. Then, just as quickly, she became Matthews again.

Bracha entered, stage right. Yehudis pretended not to notice. Bracha stood in front of the desk, waiting. Finally, she cleared her throat. Yehudis looked up.

"How often do you write your family?" Yehudis/ Matthews asked. Bracha and Yehudis had thought up this part themselves. They thought it made the whole scene more dramatic and added to the surprise of Matthews's offer. Mrs. Portnoy had agreed. The girls were quite proud of themselves.

Bracha looked at Yehudis and was surprised to see, instead of the usual twinkle, a blank, contained look in her eye. Taken aback, she fumbled her line.

"Er...um...once a week," she stuttered. *I hope she's just acting*, she thought to herself.

"And they have written to you?" Yehudis was looking somewhere over Bracha's left shoulder.

"I've only received one letter," Bracha/Lazar replied, trying to catch Yehudis's eye.

"Ladies," Mrs. Portnoy interrupted. Both girls turned to look at her. "Ladies, I'm glad that you're experimenting with your acting, but I think that the scene was good as it was."

Without thinking, Bracha said, "What?"

"I don't think you should stammer when you answer Matthews's first question," replied Mrs. Portnoy. She looked at Yehudis. "And you shouldn't be so cold.

I think the eye contact is important; Matthews has a surprise for Lazar. We're trying to build up the suspense here."

She thinks we did it on purpose! Bracha thought with amusement. She turned to share a secret smile with Yehudis, but Yehudis wouldn't look at her. *Oh, come on!* she thought. *Enough is enough!*

"Okay," she said to Mrs. Portnoy.

But it wasn't okay. It got worse and worse. And their acting suffered for it. Luckily, that day, Mrs. Portnoy was involved mostly with the other actors. Her only comment, at the end of rehearsals was: "Well, ladies. We all have our bad days. I'm sure you'll do better next time." She shook her finger playfully at them. "The show must go on!"

Bracha and Yehudis jumped down from the stage. As Bracha went for her bookbag, Esty sidled up to her. "What's with Yehudis?" she whispered curiously.

Bracha looked up, to see Yehudis disappearing through the auditorium door.

"I don't know," she said slowly. "Maybe she has a dentist's appointment or something." She didn't really want to get Esty involved.

"Well, she sure wasn't herself today," Esty declared. "And neither were you!" She wasn't going to let Bracha get off that easily.

" 'Well, lady,' " said Bracha, quoting Mrs. Portnoy, " 'we all have our bad days.' " She swung her bag over her shoulder. "I gotta run. See ya, lady."

"Everyone has to run today," Esty complained.

In contrast to her morning's walk to school, Bracha hurried home. *I wish I had someone to talk to at home,* she thought as she strode along. *We won't see Ashi until Shabbos. I could talk to my mother...but I don't want to bother her. And anyway, I'm never sure how much she understands this particular problem that I have with the family.* Bracha felt restless, and very discontented.

Home was no different than it had been for the past week or so. Moishy and Chezky had a roaring argument. It seemed that Moishy tried to kick Chezky out of the study because he wanted to study *mishnayos* there. Chezky had wanted to play with the computer.

"I can't go anywhere in this house without being disturbed!" Moishy had shouted. Bracha listened, and silently agreed.

"Or being disturbing," Yochie quipped.

"That's right!" Chezky agreed hotly.

Mrs. Baker sailed into the room and set Moishy up in her studio, with strict orders that he was not to be disturbed.

Bracha halfheartedly stuffed envelopes for half an hour. Luckily, Rachel Ahuva was cranky before dinner and Mrs. Baker asked Bracha to play with her. Bracha took her downstairs to the playroom where, wonder of wonders, no one was playing. She sat down on the rug and tried to amuse the baby with blocks. The baby rewarded her with a big smile. Bracha swept the cuddly little girl up in her arms and gave her a tight hug.

"You understand me, don't you, sweetie?"

"Ba, ba, ba," Rachel Ahuva replied.

Abba was absent from the dinner table again. Moishy sulked, Chezky complained, Tikva brooded. Things, Bracha reflected sourly, couldn't get much worse.

8

The Interview

Stuffing envelopes for Aaaaaaabba! Stuffing envelopes for Aaaaaaaabba! Stuffing envelopes for Aaaaabba!..." Yochie sang at the top of her voice.

The Baker girls were relaxing in the living room after yet another bout of campaign work. The dining room table had disappeared under mountains of envelopes and flyers. Another sea of paper surrounded the girls' feet.There were boxes here and boxes there, all filled and spilling over with stuffed envelopes. Donny and Saraleh had been given all the misprints and extras to play with, and with crayons and scissors had added to the general mess before wandering off to play somewhere else. Chezky and Moishy had also done their share. Now they were in the kitchen, doing their homework.

"Stuffing envelopes for Aaabbaaa...!"

Rivka sat up and glared at her sister.

"Yochie, if you sing that song one more time, I think I'll go crazy!"

"If I see 'Vote for Baker, I'll tell you why...' one more time, I think *I'll* go crazy," Zahava declared. "All last night I dreamed about flyers and envelopes. My eyeballs see BAKER in big red letters wherever I look."

Dini licked another envelope. "You're exaggerating," she said. "But to tell you the truth," she sighed, "I've about had it, too."

"Well, that makes it nearly unanimous," declared Yochie. "What do you 'vote,' Tikki?"

Tikva just raised her eyebrows and rolled her eyes toward the ceiling.

"I think 'the silent one' agrees," said Yochie. "Why so quiet, Tikki? Is everything okay?"

"I guess so," Tikva replied slowly. She shook her head. "Somehow this isn't going quite the way I pictured it."

"I know what you mean," agreed Dini. "Moishy still isn't being very helpful."

"And we have another 'silent one' over there," Yochie added, waving her arm in Bracha's direction. "Hey, big sister, why so talkative?"

Bracha had been staring out the window. She turned around. "Hmmm?"

"I said, why don't you let others get a word in edge-wise?"

"What are you talking about?" Bracha asked, bewildered.

"Never mind." Yochie waved an airy hand.

"Oh, leave Bracha alone," Zahava said. "She doesn't have to talk all of the time."

"True," Dini grinned. "The main thing is that she WORKS!"

"And sings!" Yochie opened her mouth to launch into her campaign song. Just then the doorbell rang.

"Saved by the bell!" Zahava exclaimed, jumping to her feet. She ran to the window to see who was there. "It's Abba. He must have forgotten his key."

"He's early!" said Bracha. She ran to the door.

"Hello, hello, hello!" shouted an exuberant Mr. Baker, bursting into the room with a huge smile. "Remember me?"

"No, who are you?" Yochie asked mock-seriously. "We're not allowed to let in strangers."

"Yochie!" Bracha glared at her sister. "Of course we remember you, Abba. Welcome home!"

Donny and Saraleh came thudding down the stairs at the sound of their father's voice. Mr. Baker barely had time to hang up his coat before they rushed into his arms. He tossed Saraleh squealing into the air, and tickled Donny till he giggled in delight. Mr. Baker turned back to the others. "Where's your mother? I have some interesting news."

"She's in the kitchen," Zahava told him.

"Kitchen ho!" cried Mr. Baker, and marched off to the back of the house, followed by the rest of the Baker clan.

He found his wife at the stove. Chezky and Moishy were doing homework at the kitchen table. Chezky jumped up to greet his father, but Moishy only rose ever so slightly and went back to his work.

"Abba, did you see what happened to the car?" Chezky asked.

Mr. Baker's expression turned serious. The car was one of his works of art. When the campaign started he had organized the older members of the family to decorate the "Campaign Mobile." "It should be tasteful but effective," he had instructed. This had been followed by an hour of sticking bumper stickers and bunting all over the Baker station wagon. Mr. Baker had even contrived a box to be set on top of the car. A small wire ran from the box to the inside of the car, where it ended in a button. When the button was pushed a sign popped up that said "BAKER" in big letters. The children loved it. Mrs. Baker refused to drive in it.

"What happened to the car?" asked Mr. Baker.

"It got left out in the rain," said Chezky.

"All the bunting ran and the car is covered with colored streaks," added Moishy.

"And the box sign doesn't work," said Donny.

"Oh, is that all?" Mr. Baker said gaily. "You had me scared for a minute there. Don't worry, there's been no lasting damage. We'll get it fixed up in no time." He turned to Mrs. Baker. "And how are you?"

"Well, well, Mr. Baker in person!" Mrs. Baker said with a big smile. "What a surprise!"

Mr. Baker gave a broad grin. "Not as surprised as you're going to be!" He walked over to the small shelf near the sink, rubbing his hands. He inclined his head toward the radio. "Got batteries for that thing?"

Mrs. Baker looked startled. "No, I don't think so. I suppose someone could run down to the corner and get some...."

"It doesn't need batteries," Moishy interrupted. "You just plug it in. What do you need it for anyway?"

Mr. Baker crossed his arms and leaned against the counter. "Because, in precisely one hour and" — he glanced at his watch — "and twenty-seven minutes, you will be able to hear your father being interviewed by John Cooperman on 'The Cooperman Hour'!"

"No!" "Really?" "Wow!" the children exclaimed. Mr. Baker looked modestly at his nails.

"Oh, Abba, how neat! What did he look like? What did you say?" Everyone was talking at once.

"I spoke about the campaign, about myself, and my background." He grinned broadly at all of them. "And about you!"

"Can we listen to it?" Zahava asked eagerly.

"You betcha!" said Mr. Baker. He snapped his fingers. "I have an idea! Let's order a couple of pizzas from Ben-Levi's. We'll sit and listen and eat pizza."

Donny whooped. Chezky and Moishy — his sulk-iness forgotten for the moment — joined hands and danced around the kitchen. Rivka, Dini, Zahava, and Bracha talked excitedly together. Tikva hugged herself with excitement. Yochie turned to her mother, cheeks flushed with glee.

"Don't you think that we ought to tape it?" she asked. "To keep it forever!"

"Smart girl!" exclaimed Mrs. Baker. "Besides, Ashi isn't here and I know he'll want to hear it."

By the time the pizzas were delivered, soda bottles opened, a blank CD found, and the CD player set up, it was time to tune in.

Moishy leapt over to the radio and turned it on — full blast.

"MOISHY!" The girls shrieked and covered their ears, except for Yochie, who shouted: "Louder, we can't hear!"

"Yochie!"

Moishy adjusted the volume. "Sorry, folks."

"Shh!" Mrs. Baker shushed.

"...and I have here in my studio tonight, Ephraim Baker," said the voice of John Cooperman.

"That's Abba!" Donny said in a loud whisper.

"Shhhhh!"

"Mr. Baker is one of the candidates for councilman in the special election to be held in a few weeks' time in Bloomfield. The other candidates include...."

"Ima!"

"Shhh, Saraleh. What is it?"

"Ima, I have to...."

"SHHHHH!"

Mrs. Baker quietly took Saraleh out of the room.

"Oh, poor Ima, she'll miss everything!" whispered Dini. She went out after her mother. There was a hushed argument in the hall. Soon they were all back.

"You haven't missed anything. Abba hasn't said a thing yet," Moishy told them.

"Shhh!"

"So Mr. Baker, tell us something about yourself..." said the voice from the radio.

"First of all, Mr. Cooperman, I'd like to thank you for having me on the show."

"That doesn't sound a bit like Abba!" said Zahava.

"Yes it does!" Bracha declared.

"No it doesn't!"

"SHHH!"

"I'm originally from New York City — Brooklyn, actually. When I was eighteen my family moved to Baltimore, which is where I received most of my post-high school education. It's also where I met my wife, a native of that city. When our oldest was twelve we moved here to Bloomfield."

"How many children did you say you had, Mr. Baker?"

"Actually, I haven't said yet. I have twelve."

"Twelve!"

"Yes, twelve. Numbers three through seven are quintuplets."

"Quintuplets!"

"Yes."

"Then you are the father of the famous Baker Quintuplets?"

"That's right, that's me!"

"Well," chortled the radio voice. "That makes your family a real 'Baker's Dozen.' "

"I guess it does," Mr. Baker's voice chuckled in polite agreement.

"I can't believe how many people make that same joke!" whispered Dini. Moishy, Chezky, and Yochie made retching noises.

"I really admire the way Abba made it look like it was the first time he'd ever heard that joke," said Bracha.

"Shh!"

The pizzas were finished quickly, and the family listened quietly for a while. Mrs. Baker's gaze was fixed on Mr. Baker as she listened, her face a happy glow. Mr. Baker looked at the radio. Bracha bit her fingernails. Zahava twirled a long strand of hair round and round her finger. Dini and Rivka looked at the radio. Chezky and Donny played a game of "hands" while Yochie laughed quietly. Moishy glared at his brothers. He put his hand over theirs and held tight. They struggled free. Saraleh put her hand on top of his. He clucked his tongue and shook his head furiously. "Nu!" he whispered. Yochie giggled.

"Shhhhhhh!" Everyone stared at the radio.

"...That's what we're trying to achieve," said Mr. Baker's voice. "Of course the ideas that are the basis of my campaign and my promises for the future are based on the foundation of hard work. There is very little that can be achieved without hard work, and much that can be achieved with it. As it says in the Talmud: 'If someone says that he has worked and found, believe him.' "

"Hear, hear!" said Yochie.

"Will you be quiet?" Moishy glared at her.

"Shh!"

"I understand that your party has a rally coming up, Mr. Baker?"

"That's right, Mr. Cooperman. We'll be having a big campaign rally a week from Monday. The governor will be there, as well as several other officials including...."

"A week from Monday!" exclaimed Bracha. She sat straight up, her eyes wide with shock. "But you can't — it can't — my —"

"Shhhhhh!"

"But...."

"It's almost finished, Bracha," Mr. Baker whispered, a finger to his lips.

Bracha stared at him and slumped in her place.

"Well, Mr. Baker," said the voice from the radio. "I'm afraid that's all the time we have. On behalf of the entire staff of the 'John Cooperman Hour,' I'd like to thank you for coming today."

"You're welcome, Mr. Cooperman, it was a pleasure."

"Good-bye, and good luck! In case you've just tuned in, we've just completed an interview with Mr. Ephraim Baker. And now...."

Mr. Baker switched off the radio.

"Abba, he didn't finish. Maybe there's more!" Zahava jumped up to switch the radio back on.

"No, honey, that's all. I know, I was there." Mr. Baker turned to the family. "Well, folks, what do you think?"

"I think you did a great job!" Yochie praised.

"Yes, dear," agreed Mrs. Baker. "You were really wonderful. We're all very proud of you!"

"Mr. Cooperman sounds like a nice man," said Dini.

"Yes," replied Mr. Baker. "We got along very well."

"A radio studio must look really neat," Moishy said wistfully. "I wish I could have been there."

"It would have been fun," agreed Mr. Baker. "Anyway, you'll all be at the rally with me, right on the podium!"

"Wow!" Chezky shouted.

"What should I wear?" wondered Zahava.

"In front of all of those people?" Dini shivered. "I'm scared!"

"I'm with Dini," said Tikva. "Just thinking about it is making me nervous."

"It's really no different than being in a play," Rivka assured her. "You've been on stage before.

In fact, Bracha is going to be on stage soon." She turned to her older sister. "You're not nervous, are you, Bracha?"

Bracha sat stiffly in her chair, arms crossed, shoulders hunched, lips pressed tightly together, with tears streaming down her cheeks.

"Bracha!" exclaimed Mrs. Baker. "Whatever is the matter?"

Bracha glared at her family. "What's the matter?" she sniffed. "What's the matter! Only that my play is a week from Monday — which just happens to be the same night as Abba's big rally!" She stared straight ahead, trying to hold in her tears.

The family stared at her dumbly. No one could think of a thing to say.

Mr. Baker cleared his throat. "Well," he said. "Well, I couldn't have gone to your play anyway. Fathers aren't usually welcome at these things."

Bracha looked at her father with hurt eyes. "And what about the rest of the family?" She glanced at her sisters and mother, glowering.

Mr. Baker sat with his head in his hands. "This is a tough one," he said. Suddenly, he straightened up. "How's about we video the play? Why not? I could hire someone to video the whole thing. Then we could all view it at our leisure. What do you say?"

Bracha looked at her father. She felt like she was going to explode. Abba just didn't understand.

She couldn't talk. She just couldn't say yes, but she

didn't want to hurt his feelings by saying no. She managed a small smile.

"Good!" Satisfied, Mr. Baker rubbed his hands. "That settles it!"

"I'm glad we could find a solution," said Mrs. Baker. But she didn't sound convinced. She turned to Bracha to say something, just as Moishy shouted: "Hey!"

"What?"

"The CD player was still on!"

"That's so funny!" giggled Yochie. "Well, Ashi can't complain that we left him out. He can hear the whole thing — every single word!"

"He sure can," muttered Bracha, hunching lower in her seat. "I'll bet he gets a real kick out of it, too."

9
Tikva's Diary #2

Dear Diary,

Here we are again! I'd like to ask how you are, but it's really a silly question to ask a book with a little writing and a lot of blank pages. Maybe I'll ask when you're all filled up and you can answer: "Good!" Ha, ha, ha!

It's been a week full of ups and downs, like a roller coaster. It's been exciting, scary, and some parts made me feel a little queasy.

We've been working very hard on the campaign. After we finished stuffing those envelopes we all went to hand them out, mostly in people's mailboxes, though Yochie and Chezky also insisted on handing them to people we passed on the street. Rivka and Dini were so embarrassed that they said they wouldn't stay with us *any longer. I suggested that anyway it would make more sense to split up the streets. So we quickly split up into two groups, one for the short blocks and one for the long.*

Our group was about halfway down the first block when Rivka asked where Saraleh and Donny were. Dini and I thought that they were with the others, but Rivka wasn't sure, so we had to go looking for them. It turned out that Mrs. Horowitz, Saraleh's teacher who lives on Vine Street, had invited all of the other group in for lemonade. By the time we found them we were almost hysterical with worry.

Zahava just finished her lemonade and said she didn't know why we were so worried. Rivka waited till we were outside on the sidewalk before shrieking back that Donny and Saraleh always run away, so why shouldn't we be worried? Then Yochie, as a joke, told them to run away, and waited until they were halfway down the block before she told us. We all ran after them, yelling our heads off. Luckily they both know not to cross the street by themselves so they stopped at the corner. Then we split up again, but we'd gone three blocks out of our way so everything took five times as long!

We got home just in time for dinner. Normally this wouldn't be so bad, but it happened that that night the mayor was supposed to come over.

We all ate like lightning and cleaned up like mad and got changed and tried to stay clean. This didn't work so well for Chezky and Donny, who had to change their shirts and brush their hair again. Then the baby figured out how to open her bottle and got apple juice all over Ima. She threw the baby at Bracha and ran up to change. It seems that there was a lot of apple juice on the baby that we didn't notice, because Bracha threw the baby at Rivka and yelled, "Change her clothes!" and then she ran up to change. A few minutes later the doorbell rang and everyone came charging downstairs trying to look normal and like all they had been doing was sitting around.

It wasn't the mayor at the door. It was Yochie. She thought it was funny. We didn't. Then the doorbell rang again. This time it was the mayor! He is a very nice man — we had a lot of fun. And amazingly, everyone stayed clean.

That wasn't the only adventure this week. We went to the main fire station. It was what Abba calls a publicity visit. We got a grand tour of the place; we saw absolutely everything. And then we got to ride on the fire truck! Of course we had our pictures taken standing around Abba and smiling for all we were worth, and we were in the papers again.

You'd think with all this excitement people around here would be very happy. But it's not so. Moishy is still barely speaking to Abba. Sometimes this gets him yelled at, but most of the time Abba doesn't seem to notice. He's so busy these days.

We hardly see Bracha anymore. I guess she should be busy, too, with the play coming up and everything, but I don't know.... She's hardly ever around. And even when she is around, she's very quiet.

I talked it over with Dini and the others. Dini thought Bracha was upset about the problem with her play and the rally being on the same night. We tried to talk to her about it but she won't talk. She's not grouchy or anything — she just keeps saying it's okay, she understands, she doesn't expect anyone to come and she doesn't want to talk about it.

She's being very brave — but I wonder if she isn't a better actress than anyone ever realized....

10
Moishy's Mess

Moishy slowly poked his head through the kitchen door and looked around. Miracle of miracles, no one was there! Quickly he slid through the door and up to his room. He knew it was empty because Chezky had baseball practice and Donny was with Ima, getting new shoes. He flopped down on his bed. He needed the privacy, he needed time to think.

What was Abba doing in school today?

I would have missed him, Moishy thought, *if I hadn't had happened to look out the window. Did it have something to do with the campaign? Or was Chezky in trouble again? Or...is it me?*

Moishy turned over in bed and rested his head in his hands. *If Abba spoke to the rebbe, maybe Rabbi Weinreb told him about that Chumash test. Not that*

85% is such a bad mark, but seeing that I usually get 95% to 100% maybe it doesn't look so good. But then again, nobody did so well on that test....

Or maybe he told Abba about all the homework I've been forgetting. But that wasn't all my fault. I mean, was I supposed to stay home and do homework when everyone went to the fire station?

Moishy turned over on his back and gazed up at the ceiling. Really, 85% wasn't so bad. It sure was a lot better than last year. Moishy shuddered as he remembered the long talks and scoldings he'd gotten about his marks last year, and the year before....

"Moishy, you're such a smart boy, we know you can do better."

"Moishy, you are not leaving this house until you do all of your work!"

"Moishy, how can this be — 97% on one test and 45% on the next? You're not trying!"

That was until Rabbi Weinreb. Rabbi Weinreb made you want to learn! He made everything he taught sound so interesting. You could see that he really loved Torah. And he really seemed to care.

Moishy sat up in bed. *That's why I want this M.V.B. award,* he said to himself. *I want Rabbi Weinreb to be proud of me.* He wrapped his hands around his knees and rocked back and forth. *And I think I've got a pretty good chance.* His eyes went to his bookbag where his Mishnah was. *I've memorized 212 mishnayos! Not bad, my boy, not bad!*

He swung his legs over the side of the bed. *I'm not really in such bad shape. One Chumash test isn't going to blow it for me. And really, 85% isn't so bad. When Abba sees the test he'll realize it was one of the harder ones.*

Moishy went rigid on the edge of the bed. *When Abba sees the test!* he thought. *And when do I ever see Abba? How come he has time to go to my school, and no time to see me!*

Moishy stood up. "I want a drink!" he said to himself, and went downstairs.

Still no one in the kitchen. *Good again,* thought Moishy. *I'll have a nice, quiet snack and then go back upstairs to work on mishnah 213!*

Moishy poured himself a drink, helped himself to some cookies and sat at the table. He decided not to use a plate so he wouldn't leave a dirty plate for someone to wash. *A paper napkin is much more efficient,* he thought.

Suddenly, he heard steps outside. At first he was annoyed. *So much for my private party,* he groaned to himself. *But, I shall rise above the occasion and greet the intruder with a smile.* He arranged his features and turned to the door.

"Abba!"

"Just the man I want to see!" said Mr. Baker, removing his gloves. "How are you, Moishy?"

Moishy gulped. *"Baruch Hashem,* Abba, I'm fine. What — what are you doing home?"

Mr. Baker's reply floated back over his shoulder as he went down the hall to hang up his coat. "I have such a crazy schedule lately that whenever I see that I have some time I snatch the chance to come home." He came back to the kitchen. "With a family as big as ours I usually bump into someone. I see you have a drink; I think I'll make myself a cup of coffee and join you." Mr. Baker turned on the coffee maker. "If you aren't busy, I'd like to have a little talk with you."

Moishy swallowed. This was what he'd been afraid of. "I was just going to do some work upstairs, but I'll talk with you first if you want, Abba."

"Good!" Mr. Baker poured himself a cup of coffee, added milk and sugar, and sat down.

"I had to be at your school today to talk to the administrator. Campaign stuff. Politics. Anyway, while I was there, since it was during your break I thought I'd stop in and see your rebbe." He looked at Moishy. Moishy looked back. Moishy licked his lips.

"What did my rebbe have to say?" he asked finally.

"Quite a lot, actually," said Mr. Baker. "First of all, he was very pleased with you. He said you were enthusiastic about the work, that you participated in class, and that you knew more *mishnayos* by heart than any other student."

Moishy couldn't enjoy this praise, as he was waiting for what was coming. He knew his parents' method: first came the good stuff, then the not-so-good stuff.

He thought the method was good as far as ways of scolding your kids went, but he wished his father would get it over with already.

"However," continued Mr. Baker.

Aha! thought Moishy.

"However, there were some things that needed to be discussed. The rebbe says that lately things don't seem to be going so well with you. He says that you're not paying attention in class, that you've missed homework assignments and that you got a lower than expected mark on the last Chumash test...."

Not paying attention in class! thought Moishy. *What does he mean? I did use some time to memorize mishnayos when there wasn't much happening, but I didn't think Rebbe noticed.*

"Well, Moishy," asked Mr. Baker. "What's up?"

"Um, well, I did mess up on some homework...."

"Why's that?"

"One time was when we went to the fire station, and then the mayor came...."

"Yes?"

"And once there were some tough questions and I didn't know the answers...."

"There was no one who could help you?"

Moishy felt the resentment rise in his chest. "You weren't home!"

Mr. Baker raised his eyebrows. "I don't see that anyone else in the family is unable to keep up with their work because I'm not here."

Moishy's face creased with scorn. "A bunch of girls! They hardly need the help I need."

"We're getting off the point," interrupted Mr. Baker. "And what about the test?"

"I didn't do so badly on that test," Moishy said defensively. "I still got one of the better marks in the class. It wasn't such an easy test. If you'd seen it —"

"The rebbe showed me a copy. It didn't strike me as something that you should have had any trouble with."

Moishy looked down at the floor. He felt all tangled up inside. He didn't want to be having this conversation with his father. When he got the M.V.B. award, then Abba would see how well he was doing.

"Moishy," Mr. Baker said gravely. "I don't want any repeat performances of last year."

Moishy looked up, horrified. *Last year was last year*, he thought. That was over now.

"So what are you going to do about all this, son?"

Moishy exploded in anger. "Do? What's there to do? With all of the chaos in the house, and you never home? What am I supposed to do?" Tears streamed down his cheeks.

Mr. Baker looked at his son, a carefully neutral look on his face. "Is the campaign really interfering with your life so much?" he asked.

Moishy sniffed. "I don't know."

"Well," said Mr. Baker, gently placing a hand on his son's shoulder, "I see there's more here than meets the eye. Let's stop this discussion for now." Mr. Baker got up and put his cup in the sink. "The campaign won't be too much longer. Once it's over I should have regular hours again and then we can work all this out. Okay?"

"Okay, Abba."

Mr. Baker left the kitchen. Moishy got up and rinsed his cup. On an afterthought he rinsed his father's cup and saucer, too. He wiped the table and threw away his paper napkin. Then he went upstairs.

He took out his Mishnah and sat down at his desk.

He stared at the page without seeing the words. With an effort he pushed the talk with his father out of his mind. He began to memorize mishnah number 213.

It didn't go as easily as the others. Somehow, the taste had gone out of things.

11
Stage Fright

Butterflies! Big, fat butterflies with huge wings! Not to mention the moths — huge, fluttering creatures that wouldn't stand still for a second. *That's what I feel in my stomach*, thought Bracha. *I never thought I'd be so nervous, but here I am. How am I ever going to make it through the day?*

Bracha was enjoying a private moment. Her inner alarm had woken her early this morning, though it was just the day she'd been hoping to sleep later than usual. This was the day of the play and she didn't want to be overtired. No luck! She was awake before all the rest. She and her butterflies!

Well, there sure was enough to think about...or rather, brood about. Her relationship with Yehudis had gone from bad to worse. Bracha was still annoyed at Yehudis's reaction to her complaint.

Not surprisingly, their rehearsals had also been terrible. How can you act with a person who is barely speaking to you? The missed cues and mumbled lines had nearly driven poor Mrs. Portnoy to distraction.

And, on top of that, for days Bracha would come late so as to have an excuse not to speak with Yehudis before rehearsal. She did this until Mrs. Portnoy caught on and spoke to her about her tardiness.

"Team spirit!" the director had chirped. "That's even more important than good acting. Tardiness can't be tolerated."

Even as Bracha began arriving promptly again, Yehudis was contributing her own brand of trouble. She got into the habit of leaving the auditorium the second rehearsal was over. A couple of times she missed hearing important instructions for the next rehearsal. Once she even missed a rehearsal entirely because she didn't stay to hear that the time was changed. Mrs. Portnoy really blew up over that one!

Finally, one afternoon she'd kept the both of them after rehearsal and gave them a good talking-to. She spoke about how this had the potential to be the best play Bais Yaakov of Bloomfield ever put on, about how it had an important and universal message. She spoke about how it was a privilege to be in a school play and the actors were chosen, not only for their acting ability, but also for their ability to keep up with their school work — *and* to get along with people.

"Ladies," she had said soberly, "I feel I can be very frank with you. The way the two of you are behaving now is undermining the success of this play. You are too old to be babied. If you don't shape up I'm afraid I'll have to find someone else for your parts."

That had done it. Bracha and Yehudis had left that meeting with eyes averted and ears ringing. There was a marked improvement in their performances and overall behavior at rehearsal. Bracha sighed. Their relationship was harder to repair.

She turned over restlessly in bed. *I wish I knew what to do*, she thought in frustration. *When I think about it honestly, it was really all my doing. It's not Yehudis's fault that my family is so much fun. I really should be happy about that. And happy that I have them...*

She considered getting out of bed, even though it was still early. Then she fell back on her pillow. The thought of the whole long day stretched out ahead filled her with dread. Not only would it be an eternity until tonight — when she would be on stage, performing at last — but she would have to endure "rally talk" all day, too. It was bad enough that the rally was the same night as her play. She didn't want to hear about it all day long besides.

If only it had been one day before, she thought for what must have been the millionth time, or one day after...or even in the afternoon. She'd have liked to go to the rally, too....

"Good morning, Bracha, darling," Yochie trilled, sticking her head through the doorway. "Big day today, huh?"

Bracha gave a noncommittal grunt.

"I beg your pardon?" Yochie put her cupped hand up to her ear.

"I'm saving my voice," Bracha informed her.

"Whuffor? Oh right, the play! Wow! Good luck!" Yochie smiled and flitted out of the room.

Oh boy, thought Bracha in rising indignation. *She didn't even remember my big night! Well, I'm not going to put up with this all day!* She threw off her covers and leapt out of bed. It was only a matter of minutes before she was dressed and running headlong down the stairs to the kitchen.

"Ima!" she cried as she burst into the kitchen.

Mrs. Baker sat at the table with a cup of coffee and a bagel. Donny and Saraleh were busy listening to their breakfast cereal, which wasn't easy with the baby merrily banging a cup with a spoon right beside them.

"Good morning, Bracha," Mrs. Baker greeted her. "Cold cereal this morning, I'm afraid. Life is too hectic for a fancier breakfast today. Kinderlach, stop listening to your breakfast and start eating it."

"You have a bagel," said Bracha.

Mrs. Baker looked down at her plate. "Too true," she said. "Shall I microwave one for you, too?"

"No, it's okay," Bracha muttered, waving a hand. Who could think of food on a day like this?

"I once read somewhere that on the day of a big performance, actors don't eat much," her mother said, as if reading her thoughts. "It seems that the wrong foods can affect the voice. But I don't expect that that's a realistic expectation to have of a growing girl." Mrs. Baker grinned at her daughter. "At least, I hope it isn't."

"Don't worry, Ima, I'll eat. Or I'll try, anyway. I'm not sure that I have much room in my tummy with all of these butterflies fluttering around in there." Bracha patted her stomach.

"Are you worried about anything in particular?" asked Mrs. Baker.

"Yes. Well, no. Well, what I mean is that everything looks like it should be good but you really never know until it happens — if you know what I mean."

"Hmm," Mrs. Baker agreed. "I think I do."

"Anyway," Bracha continued. "Today is a short day at school, and I thought I'd spend the day at Esty's house. We could go over things one more time and get dressed together and stuff. And I could leave from there."

"Why would you want to do that?"

"Well," said Bracha. "Things will be so busy here,

getting ready for the rally and all...I thought that it would be easier..." she ended lamely.

Mrs. Baker looked doubtful. "We'd like to see you in your costume..." she began.

"I know," Bracha hurried on. "But you can see it after the show and all you want on the video. And I don't think anyone here is really going to have much time...." *Please, Ima*, she thought, *please don't make me stay. I couldn't stand it!*

"Well, Bracha," said Mrs. Baker reluctantly. "If this is what you think is best, I won't object."

"Yes, I do, Ima. Thanks!"

"Good, then." There was a clatter of footsteps on the stairs. "I hear the rest of the crew, so give me a hug for luck, Bracha. Quick, before they come." Mrs. Baker held out her arms.

As Bracha hugged her mother she thought about how much she loved her and how understanding she was. She'd had a silly little hope that she'd wake up this morning and find out that her mother was coming to the play after all. But she knew that really wasn't possible. Her mother was doing what she had to do. Her place was by Abba's side.

"Thank you, Ima," she whispered as the rest of the family came into the kitchen.

Sitting through class that morning was not easy. Even knowing that it was a short day didn't help. Bracha tried not to look at Yehudis every five minutes, but it was hard. Once, when she gave in and peeked, she caught Yehudis looking at *her*! Both of them looked away quickly, but Bracha felt a flutter of hope in her heart, quite different from the dance of the butterflies in her stomach....

A large group of girls clustered around Bracha and Esty on their walk home. Yehudis was nowhere to be seen. She must, Bracha surmised, have gone home by a different route — to avoid her. Her spirits sank again. She tried to attend to the girls' talk.

"I couldn't eat breakfast this morning," Esty announced. "And I don't know how in the world I'm going to manage lunch."

"Me neither!" Bracha agreed fervently.

"Really?" asked Miriam Wexler. "I'm just the opposite. When I'm nervous I get even more hungry."

"Not me," said Esty. "I feel like I'm going to throw up!"

"But it's hours until the play," Shani Baum pointed out.

"You're right," Esty reconsidered. "I'll wait until just before."

"No, don't do that!" Bracha blurted, with real worry.

Everyone laughed.

"Okay, 'Moses,' I'll hold off for you."

"Bracha, how about an interview for the *B.Y. Times*?" suggested Shani. The editor of the school newspaper was already rummaging in her schoolbag for a pen and notebook.

"It's a deal," Bracha said promptly. "After the play, though." Nervously, she added, "*If* it comes out good."

"Oh, it will," Shani assured her. "Let's meet at the pizza shop tomorrow for the interview. We'll have the Ben-Levi special, with lots of gooey cheese, and olives, and mushrooms...."

"*Don't!*" moaned Bracha and Esty in unison, clutching their stomachs.

The group separated with a lot of laughter and good wishes. Bracha and Esty walked on to Esty's house alone. At the door, Esty paused.

"Are you sure you want to spend all afternoon at my house?" she asked Bracha.

"Yes," Bracha said. She stared straight ahead. "I'm really trying to be a good sport about all of this. Anyway, we've talked about this all week and I don't want to talk about it anymore." Bracha realized that she might be speaking too harshly. She turned to her friend. "You understand, don't you?"

"Yeah, I do. And I think you're being terrific. I don't think I could have been as good as you."

Bracha made no answer. Esty glanced at her, sideways. "Are you and Yehudis still not talking?"

"Who said we're not talking?" Bracha asked quickly.

"No one in particular," said Esty, looking up at the sky. "I didn't mean that you weren't talking, exactly. But lately things seem a little cool between the two of you."

"I don't think I want to talk about it," Bracha replied.

Esty shrugged. "Fine with me. Come on, let's go in."

The girls spent the afternoon practicing, talking and noshing. Despite the butterflies, Bracha managed a decent lunch. She didn't do too badly on the potato chips, either, until she told Esty what her mother had said that morning.

"Oh no!" Esty said. She grabbed at her throat. "Do you think we've ruined our voices by eating too much?"

"I hope not," replied Bracha. "Here, you sing one of your songs and then I'll sing one of mine, and we'll see."

Esty sang first. Bracha assured her that her voice was as fine as ever. Privately, though, she felt that it wasn't quite as important for Esty as it was for her. Esty didn't have a lead part.

"Go on now," Esty urged. "You sing."

As Bracha sang the familiar words, she wondered if Yehudis knew about food and voices.

"Sounds good to me," Esty declared.

"Well, I'm not risking anything else. Let's put all of this nosh away before we're tempted to finish it off."

As they were cleaning up, Esty's mother came into the room.

"Young women who have big performances must have naps in the afternoon," she announced.

"Oh, Ima," Esty groaned, obviously embarrassed.

Esty's mother was adamant. Bracha found herself on a bottom bunk with Esty on the top, under strict orders not to talk, but to sleep. *I'm glad my mother wouldn't make me do this*, Bracha thought. Unexpected tears pricked her eyes as she thought longingly of home. *Oh well*, she sighed. *I know I won't sleep a wink, but I might as well close my eyes and get it over with....*

Bracha awoke with a start.

Wow, she thought, *I did it. I actually fell asleep! I wonder what time it is?* The window was tightly curtained. She felt a clutch of panic. *What if I slept through the play? Esty's mother wouldn't let something like that happen...I hope.* She climbed out of bed.

"Esty!" she called softly at the upper bunk. "Esty, wake up!"

There was no sound. Anxiously she peered over the edge of her friend's bed.

No Esty!

Bracha felt panic rising in her chest. She went to the door and tried to open it. It was locked!

She knocked. "Hello! Hello?" she called. "Esty, let me out of here! This isn't funny!"

She heard voices out in the hall. "It sounds like she woke up!" she heard Esty say in a loud, excited whisper. "You go down to the kitchen and we'll be there soon."

Whoever she'd spoken to slipped quietly downstairs. Esty opened the door.

"Sorry about the locked door," she said cheerfully. "We had to make sure we'd know when you woke up."

"What are you talking about?" Bracha demanded.

"It's time," said Esty importantly. "For the big pow-wow."

"What big pow-wow? What are you talking about? What time is it, anyway?"

"Don't worry, we have plenty of time," Esty told her. "Now we go to the big shalom pow-wow." She turned and went down the stairs.

"Esty, what are you up to?" Bracha asked as she trotted after her. She was confused and angry. What was going on?

When they got downstairs Esty stood in the kitchen door, blocking Bracha's view. "Out! Everyone out!" she commanded. "Except you, of course," she said to someone Bracha couldn't see.

A stream of Esty's little brothers and sisters pushed past them, followed by Esty's mother, wiping her hands on her apron. "Have a nice snack, dear — but don't ruin your dinner," was all she said.

Bracha and Esty stepped into the empty kitchen. Empty, that is, except for someone sitting at the kitchen table.

"Yehudis!" exclaimed Bracha. Yehudis and Bracha stared at each other.

"Bracha, sit down," Esty commanded. "I'll make the tea. We can't have cocoa, you know, because of our voices." Bracha sat down slowly across from Yehudis. Esty continued speaking as she puttered around the kitchen. "I enjoy being one of the *talmidos shel Aharon*," she said, referring to those peacemakers who follow in the footsteps of Aharon HaKohen. "And since you people sure need my services, I decided to maneuver this little meeting. A shalom pow-wow."

"A shalom pow-wow," Bracha repeated mechanically, still staring at Yehudis.

"That's right." Esty set down steaming cups of tea. "And we won't leave this table until everything is worked out!" She crossed her arms. "*Beli neder!*" she added hastily.

The girls said *brachos* and sipped their tea. Finally Bracha cleared her throat.

"Yehudis," she said huskily. "Yehudis, I'm sorry. It wasn't your fault. I shouldn't have involved you with my problems with my family. And it was really childish to let things drag on the way they did.... It was silly pride, really. I hope you can forgive me because even though I haven't acted that way, I really treasure our friendship. Will you forgive me?"

"Oh, Bracha!" Yehudis choked out. "What's there to forgive? Last night I had a long talk with a cousin of mine, who has nine brothers and sisters. I was being so closed-minded! I was so busy thinking about what I don't have — I never thought that *having* could be hard, too!"

"It's actually not half as hard as I make it out to be," Bracha admitted. "I really shouldn't feel so sorry for myself."

"Live and learn," said Esty. Her voice was slow and deep. The other two girls looked at her. She had her glasses down her nose and was looking very pompous, as Mrs. Portnoy had trained her to do. Yehudis smiled broadly. Then Bracha giggled. Soon all three of them were rolling with laughter.

Esty produced doughnuts from the microwave. All dangers to the voice forgotten, the girls ate with gusto and talked. It was as if nothing bad had ever happened.

Yehudis tapped on the side of her cup with her spoon. "Attention," she said. "Attention, please! I would like to propose a toast!" She raised her almost empty cup. "To one of the *talmidos shel Aharon* — Esty. May you have many more pow-wows!"

"*Lechaim, lechaim!*" chorused Esty and Bracha, clinking cups. Bracha felt relaxed and warm inside. She had her friend back. Then her eye lit on the clock ticking placidly away above the kitchen counter. "Oh no, look at the time!" she nearly shrieked. "We have to start getting ready!"

The butterflies were back, in full force.

The girls left an hour before the family in order to put on costumes and makeup early. They weren't taking any chances.

As they walked through the auditorium door they had to stop short in admiration.

The stage was set with the scenery for the first scene, the courtroom. A tall desk had been set up for Esty, as the judge. There was a table for the officials of the court and a sort of a fence for Moses Lazar to stand in as he was sentenced. The backdrop was painted to look like a crowded courtroom with rows of interested spectators sitting in a gallery. Below the stage, to the right, was the piano. Someone had thoughtfully put a small vase of flowers on top. It added a gay note.

To the left was an easel bearing a stack of placards. The top one said "Legacy of Gold" in beautiful letters. The placards would be used to announce the acts. There were also programs on each chair.

"Oh, isn't this exciting!" Esty whispered.

"I think we're the first ones here," Yehudis whispered back.

"No, we're not," said Bracha. "There's Mrs. Portnoy." Her heart pounded as she started down the aisle. She could hardly believe this was real. It felt as make-believe as...as the stage setting. But all too soon these empty rows would be filled with people, all waiting to be entertained for two hours by her — Bracha Baker!

Mrs. Portnoy came toward them at a trot, beaming. "I knew I could count on you to be the first, girls," she said. "Hurry around backstage, now. Costumes and makeup are going to take some time. We want to do a really professional job. Especially" — she winked at Bracha and Yehudis — "on our stars!"

Soon, the whole cast was there. The tension in the air was so thick, Yehudis declared, you could practically cut it with a knife.

"Milchig or fleishig?" jittered Esty.

"Stay still," said Mrs. Portnoy's niece. She was a beautician and came to help with the makeup. She had a book on theater makeup with her, and leafed through it from time to time.

"I don't see why I need makeup," protested Bracha. "Most of my face is covered with a beard."

"We need to make you look more like a man," Mrs. Portnoy's niece said firmly, as she darkened Bracha's eyebrows.

Esty put on her judge's wig. She looked at herself in the mirror and simpered, "Didn't I see you in the Georgie catalogue?"

The nervous cast exploded with laughter. "Not the Georgie catalogue," someone shouted. "The JUDGIE catalogue!"

Bracha laughed until tears ran down her face.

"Careful," warned the beautician, wiping her own eyes. "You'll smear your makeup."

The scariest time, in Bracha's opinion at least, was after everyone and everything was ready. It was still fifteen minutes to curtain time. The girls took turns peeking through the crack in the curtain to pass the time.

"There's Rebbetzin Falowitz!" cried Esty during her turn. "And she's brought her mother!"

"Really? Let me see!" the other girls cried.

"My turn," said Yehudis. Esty moved away. Yehudis put her eye to the crack.

"Careful," Bracha said in a shrill whisper. "They'll see you!"

Yehudis put her finger to her lips. "There's my mother and sister. Rebbetzin Falowitz is speaking with Mrs. Portnoy. Now Mrs. Portnoy's stopped talking. She's coming this way! There's a lot of people coming in now. That's funny, that looks like...."

"Ladies!" Mrs. Portnoy appeared on the stage. "Ladies, it's almost curtain time." She clapped her hands twice. "Everyone to their places. All of you look great and I'm sure everything will go just perfectly." She smiled a grand smile at them all. "Quickly, everyone to their places!"

The pianist began playing a medley of tunes from the play, as an overture and a signal for the audience to settle down. The cast could hear the mumble of voices fade and stop.

Yehudis turned to Esty. "Isn't it time for you to throw up?" she whispered.

"Shhh!" shushed Bracha with a wild look in her eye.

"Ladies," admonished Mrs. Portnoy. She gave the signal to raise the curtain. There was a sprinkling of applause from the audience.

As the narrator spoke the introduction, Bracha, from her frozen position on the stage, looked out at the audience. With the auditorium darkened and the stage lights on, all she saw was a sea of vague forms. *It wouldn't have even mattered if they were here*, she thought. *I couldn't have seen them anyway. Don't kid yourself, Bracha, you wish they were here. Oh well, the show must go on!*

And the show went on. Moses Lazar was sentenced to seven years' servitude. Bracha thought Esty did a perfect job as the judge. Then came the time for the tearful good-bye between Moses and his wife.

"Oh, Moses, Moses," cried the girl who played his wife. "Being too honest has led you to no good. Why didn't you leave that youth alone? Now you're leaving me and the children forever!" She dabbed her eyes with a handkerchief.

"Don't cry, my wife, don't cry," said Moses/Bracha. "I can't believe that Hashem would punish us for a good act. We will find out in the end that this was for the best."

"I can't see it, Moses, but you must be right. It's God's will," She gave him a ragged bag. "Here are your tallis and tefillin. Oh, Moses, are you sure this is the right thing to do? These ruffians hate Jews so much, and they'll know you're a Jew with these."

"Perhaps they should...." Moses/Bracha took a step closer. "Shalom, Rachel...."

"Go in peace, my husband." The actress that played Rachel ran off the stage in tears. The audience was rapt.

This is really going well! thought Bracha. She heard the first bars of *"Lev Tahor,"* her song. *And no one is here to see!* Tears came to her eyes as she began to sing:

"Now that she's go-oo-one
Here I stand, all alone
Fettered and sha-aa-ackled
Draped for a journey far from home
How will I live without them?
How will I last till I'm free?
The Torah and mitzvos will be my guide
I know that Hashem is with me!"

As the piano played the musical interlude before the next verse Bracha reflected that the tears probably looked pretty good.

"Lev Tahor," she continued, *"bara li, Elokim...."*

She closed her eyes and put her whole self into the song.

"Al tashlichayni, milfanecha, viruach kadshecha, al tikach mimeni...."

There was a moment of silence. Then came a whoop from the audience. *That sounds like Yochie!* thought Bracha, her eyes flying open. The applause began, and became louder and stronger. People were rising to their feet. The house lights came on and there, right in the middle of the standing ovation were — the quints! There they were clapping wildly, and cheering louder than all the rest. Just before the curtain fell, Bracha saw Yochie wave.

The moving beginning of the play led impetus to the whole evening. Scene after scene was charged with dramatic excitement, keeping the audience on the edge of their chairs. No one forgot their lines, all of the scene changes went smoothly, everyone entered and exited on cue. The applause for the curtain calls was thunderous; it went on for ten minutes! Everyone agreed that this was the best play ever put on by the Bais Yaakov of Bloomfield — possibly the best Bais Yaakov play ever.

Behind the curtain Mrs. Portnoy was wiping tears of joy from her eyes as she hugged one cast member after another. "Ladies, you were wonderful," she said over and over again. "*Baruch Hashem*, everything was perfect."

Bracha and Yehudis were giddy with happiness. As the stars of the triumph they were the center of attention.

"Oh, Bracha, you were incredible!" gushed Esty.

"*Baruch Hashem*! You were pretty good yourself, Judgie!"

"And Yehudis, so were you! When you sang that song in the fifth act I thought I'd never stop crying!"

"I was scared that I would *start* crying and I wouldn't be able to sing!"

"Did you ever throw up, Esty?" asked another girl.

"Nope," Esty replied. "I guess it's too late now."

"It certainly IS!" laughed Bracha.

There was a commotion at the stage door. In walked the Baker quints, followed by what looked like half the audience.

"Bracha!" they cried, rushing to her.

"Oh, you guys!" Bracha held out her arms to them. There was much hugging and more tears.

"I can't tell you how much I appreciate your coming," Bracha said in a suddenly shaky voice.

"If you'd only let us get a word in edgewise, you'd have known all along," Dini said pointedly.

"But you were so touchy," Yochie continued, "that we were scared to open our mouths."

"Not that we blamed you," Tikva put in hastily.

"So we decided to surprise you!" finished Rivka.

"I'm so happy," Bracha smiled. "You guys really came through for me."

"As if we would miss our sister in the play of the year!" Zahava said reproachfully.

Bracha just grinned. The quints grinned back. Yochie started clapping her hands rhythmically and chanted: "Speech! Speech!" The rest of the crowd took up the beat. Bracha's grin turned into a look of dismay.

Yehudis sidled over to her and whispered into her ear: "Come on, 'Moses,' you can do it."

Bracha cleared her throat. The chanting died down.

"Well, I guess the first thing I have to do is thank Hashem. We always say *'be'ezras Hashem,'* and with this play I know we could all feel the help we got from *Shamayim*.

"We're supposed to learn from everything that happens to us. Over the weeks of rehearsals, a person can forget that and get involved with selfish stuff. Even though a play is a group effort, people can be selfish enough to forget — because of their personal reasons — that their job is to get the show on the road. With this cast that didn't happen. We had a special bunch of girls here. And one great director, Mrs. Portnoy." Bracha gestured to the teacher, who inclined her head. There was lively applause.

"Thank you, ladies," said Mrs. Portnoy graciously, holding up a hand. "But I think Bracha has more to say."

"I guess I do." Bracha took a deep breath. "For myself, personally, I gained a bit more. First of all I gained a friend, Yehudis Klein. Yehudis was the new girl in school. Through the play, we all got to know her and the good things about her. She's not 'the new girl' anymore; she's part of the crowd, a Bais Yaakov of Bloomfield girl."

She paused, gathering her thoughts.

"And I gained one more thing. I gained deeper appreciation of my family's love for me. I haven't been easy to live with these past few weeks and no one even peeped. My sisters gave up a very big event to be here tonight...." Bracha stopped for breath. "I have to thank Hashem for letting me be part of tonight, I have to thank Him for making me a Jew, a Torah Jew. And perhaps, most of all, I have to thank Him for making me a Baker."

Cheers rose to the rafters. Someone started singing. The quints joined hands and started to dance. Everyone joined in. As Bracha danced and sang with her sisters, teachers and friends, she felt happy and loved — right down to the bottom of her heart.

12
Tikva's Diary #3

Dear Diary,

Well, I know I last wrote pretty recently, but I'm so full of feeling that I just have to write again. I don't think this diary should only be for complaining.

I can't tell you what an exciting triumph Bracha's play was! Normally, school plays are good, and fun, too — but as Ima says, "It's not exactly Broadway." And plays that are adapted from books never seem to be quite as good as the book. But last night was different. I think the difference was the performance of Bracha and Yehudis.

We walked into the auditorium and found our seats after the lights went down. This was in order that Bracha wouldn't see us. When the curtain went up and *the play started, it sounded as if it would be like any other play. The narrator said what she said and the action began. Even when Bracha entered and spoke it was like any other play. I'll admit I felt like a dutiful sister, ready to clap just because it was Bracha standing up there. Then she began her first song.*

I've never felt anything like it. Suddenly the whole audience was swept up with her, by what she was singing. I heard a woman in front of me begin to sniff and cry softly. To tell the truth, I felt like crying myself.

Standing up there on that stage, singing that song, Bracha showed us things about herself, and about Moses Lazar, that we never imagined. I really respect my sister. I don't think I could go up on stage like that and reveal myself to so many people. I don't know what it takes — maybe you just have to be very sure of yourself.

Anyway, when she finished the audience exploded! My ears are still ringing from the applause. I thought they'd clap all night. It was really something. And of course, we Bakers were the loudest of all.

As the play started, that's how it went on. Bracha and Yehudis were incredible, and they drew everyone with them into the action. Yochie described the scenery to me, and it sounded really lifelike. But even without seeing it I got completely swept up into the story. I forgot I was sitting in an auditorium in Bloomfield, and really believed I was far away in Australia!

Afterward, we all went backstage. Everyone was so excited and happy, and there was hugging and kissing and dancing and singing. I still feel like I'm flying from it all.

Of course when we got home there was more excite-ment. Ima and all the boys had gone to the rally, don't forget. They all had buttons and bumper stickers and silly hats. Ima had confetti in her sheitel. We played back the recording of Abba's speech. (Chezky said that it sounded just like what Abba said on the radio. Moishy sort of kicked him under the table, but Abba said it was all right, it was more or less what he'd said on the radio, that was the problem with political speeches. He said he'd rather say a devar Torah any time.) Then Abba in-sisted that Ima look at the video (we still had all of the equipment), and he hopped in and out of the room to watch whenever Bracha sang a solo. Ima sat riveted to the screen, and at the end she clapped her hands and gave Bracha a big hug. I get the feeling she would have rather been at the play than the rally.... I guess she'll get the "Wife of the Year" Award, even if we have to give it to her ourselves. And "Mother of the Year" too!

It seems that the organizers of the rally were a little upset that the quints didn't show. I think they expect-ed that having quintuplets there with Abba would draw more people. Abba said that he was running for office, not the quints, and if people were only voting for him because he was a novelty then he's not sure he wants to go into politics.

"Does this mean we won't be living in the White House?" Yochie asked.

You know what everyone shouted: "Yo-o-chie!"

But, seriously, we have to sit down and think about what it means to have Abba in politics. Things can seem so exciting and important on the surface, but when you're in the middle of them they can be very different. At first we thought only of the excitement and fame. You know, you could meet a new kid:

KID: What does your father do?

ONE OF US (casually): Oh, he's in politics.

You get the idea. It's like being quintuplets and being in the newspapers and stuff. It looks like fun but no one else knows how nosy and boring some interviewers can be! And talk about invasion of privacy! Sometimes we can hardly walk down the street without everyone staring.

Well, darling diary, in just a few days we'll know if Abba is in politics or not. As you can tell, I have mixed feelings. I think we all do. Well, if Ima can be so terrific about it, then we can be good kids, too.

See ya,
Tikva

13

A Surprise for Tikva

L ec-shun night! Lec-shun night!" Donny and Saraleh were bouncing on the sofa, chanting loudly. "Lec-shun night! Lec-shun night!"

"I think that's quite enough, kids," Mrs. Baker said firmly. She set down a tray filled with drinks and snacks on the coffee table. The doorbell rang. "Why don't you go and see who's at the door?"

The two children ran from the room. Zahava came in with another tray, as full as the first.

"Oh, Ima," she said. "I can't believe it's election night. I though it would never happen! Aren't you nervous?" She held her tray steady as her mother unloaded it onto the coffee table.

"A little," admitted Mrs. Baker. "But I have a lot of confidence in your father."

"Me too!" said Zahava. They both went back into the kitchen. The other girls were there. Tikva and Dini were finishing up the dinner dishes. Bracha popped popcorn, and Yochie and Rivka loaded up another tray.

"I can't believe how much food this family eats!" Yochie marveled.

"Well," said Rivka. "It is going to be a long night."

"We might not know the results until after midnight," added Tikva, her cheeks flushed with excitement.

"Ima thinks that Abba is going to win," said Zahava confidently.

"I didn't exactly say that, Zahava...." Mrs. Baker raised her eyebrows at Zahava.

"I always thought this sort of thing was *min hashamayim*," said Dini. She stopped working and looked right at her mother.

"Well, dear, it is." Mrs. Baker paused to think for a moment.

"Everything is *min hashamayim*," blurted out Yochie.

"That's true," said Mrs. Baker. "But in this world we have to do our *hishtadlus* — our work toward achieving a goal. After we've done what we're supposed to do, then we can have confidence that whatever happens is *min hashamayim*. When we tell ourselves that something is from heaven, we're saying that we've done our all, and no matter how things turn out we won't regret what we did and how we did it."

"Well, Abba certainly did his all!" said Bracha, with feeling.

Everyone agreed loudly with her.

"That's true," said Mrs. Baker. "And that's why, no matter what happens, we can be proud of him."

The kitchen door swung open and in walked a fair young man with a good-natured look on his face. Donny was swinging from his left hand, while he carried Saraleh in his right.

"Ashi!" Mrs. Baker put her hand to her mouth. "I was so distracted that I forgot I sent Donny and Saraleh to the door. I'm glad it was you and not someone else!"

"You're right, Ima. It's much worse to forget about a total stranger than your 'long lost' son." Ashi's face was serious but his eyes twinkled.

"Oh, Ashi," said Bracha. "Ima didn't mean it that way!"

"I certainly didn't!" said Mrs. Baker. "Welcome home!"

"I know you didn't, Ima!" He hugged Saraleh closer and tugged on Donny's hand. "Anyway, I had the best welcoming committee ever! Right, guys?"

Saraleh grinned from ear to ear. Donny jumped up and down and shouted, "Right!"

Mrs. Baker picked up the last tray. "Let's go into the living room and talk until Abba gets here."

Ashi eyed the tray appreciatively. "It looks like I came just in time."

"You have to share," Saraleh told him firmly.

Everyone laughed. "If you say so," said Ashi.

They all trooped into the living room, led by Mrs. Baker. Chezky was already there. He had been about to sample a dip with his index finger, which he snatched back guiltily.

"Ah, ah, ah!" Yochie shook her finger at him.

"You should talk..." began Zahava.

"*Lashon hara*," said Dini with an exaggerated whisper. She put her finger to her lips and opened her eyes wide.

"I think we can all dig in," Mrs. Baker decided. "Your father should be here any minute."

"Goody!" said Ashi.

"Goody for Abba or goody for the food?" asked Bracha, with a sidelong glance at her big brother.

"Goody for both — and in that order!" he grinned at her and began to help himself. Everyone else did, too.

The doorbell rang again. Before anyone could get up, Mr. Baker walked into the room.

"Abba!"

"Vote for Baker, I'll tell you why!" shouted Yochie.

"Hello, hello, hello!" said Mr. Baker as he waved. Bracha came and took her father's coat. "Thank you, Bracha." He looked around approvingly. "Well, this looks better than campaign headquarters."

"Bracha makes popcorn better than anyone!" shouted Donny loyally.

Mr. Baker ruffled the small boy's hair. "I'll bet

that's true," he said. "Hi, Ashi, I didn't see you there in the crowd. Welcome home!" Ashi and his father exchanged greetings.

Everyone sat down. Mr. Baker heaped his plate liberally with potato chips and dips. "Well, it's certainly been an exciting month for the Baker family," he remarked.

"I think the most exciting thing was Bracha's play," said Zahava. "That is, the most exciting thing that's happened so far," she added hastily.

"That certainly was a triumph," agreed Mr. Baker. "You see, kids, what can be achieved with hard work? Bracha spent weeks memorizing and rehearsing. Even when she suffered a major disappointment she didn't give up for a minute."

"Just like you said on the radio," said Dini.

"That's right!" Just then the phone rang. Mr. Baker went to answer it.

"Where's Moishy?" asked Mrs. Baker.

"Upstairs," answered Chezky. "I'll go and get him."

"It's funny that he's upstairs," said Yochie. "It's not like Moishy to miss all of this nosh."

"He's probably memorizing more *mishnayos*," said Rivka, offhandedly.

"I'd think he'd know all of them by now!" Yochie declared. She looked puzzled.

Mr. Baker came into the room. "Early results," he explained. "It's really too soon to tell. Things look pretty even."

"Oh, this is too exciting," said Zahava, bouncing on the sofa cushions.

"No bouncing," said Mrs. Baker absently.

"Anyway," said Mr. Baker, sitting down and taking up his plate again. "As I was saying, Bracha worked hard, very hard, and she achieved." He smiled proudly at his oldest daughter.

Moishy trailed Chezky into the room. "I found him!" Chezky said.

"Too late, the chips are all gone —" Yochie sang out.

"Yochie!" Moishy began accusingly.

"— from this bag!" Yochie looked at her brother with a mischievous grin.

"Yochie, one of these days..." Moishy let the sentence dangle. He helped himself to food and sat down on the floor next to the coffee table.

"To continue the conversation," said Mrs. Baker, "I'd also like to add how proud we are that our girls gave up going to the rally to see the play."

Mr. Baker agreed heartily.

"I'm sure we had much more fun at the play than we would ever have had at the rally," said Tikva.

"Could be," put in Ashi. "But you didn't know that at the time."

"True," said Mr. Baker. "Working on your *middos* is also hard work."

"It sure is!" chimed in Yochie.

The doorbell rang again. "Who can that be?" asked

Mr. Baker. He went to the door, followed by the younger members of the Baker clan.

Yochie ran to the window. "There's a U.P.S. van outside!" she shouted.

"Why would we be getting a package?" Mrs. Baker asked no one in particular. The rest of the family rushed to the door.

At the door was a delivery man with a large box.

"What is it?"

"Who is it for?"

Zahava bent down and read the address. "It's for Tikki!" she said, surprise and bewilderment mixing in her voice.

"For Tikki?"

"For *me*?" cried Tikva.

Mr. Baker had Tikva sign for the package. He thanked the delivery man and closed the door. Then he picked up the big box and brought it into the study. Everyone followed after him.

He scanned the sea of faces. His eyes found Tikva and his expression softened. "Come, Tikva," he said gently. "Let's see what's in this box."

"Quickly!" pleaded Chezky.

"Shhh," said Yochie.

Tikva knelt down next to Mr. Baker. Together they unwrapped the package.

"It says IBM on the box," Moishy said excitedly. "It must be for the computer!"

"You'll see," said Mr. Baker.

Inside the large box were two boxes. Mr. Baker picked up the smaller one. "Open this one first," he said, handing it to Tikva.

Tikva opened the box. Inside was a small keyboard. Instead of the usual number of keys there were six keys in a rectangle, three on the top and three on the bottom. There were also a few of the usual function keys one sees on a computer keyboard. Below the space bar was a ribbon of what looked like aluminum foil.

"What's it for?" yelled Chezky.

Moishy, in the meantime, had been skimming the pamphlet that came with the strange keyboard.

"It's for braille!" he exclaimed. "It's a keyboard for braille."

Tikva could hardly believe it. "Really?" she exclaimed softly. Behind her thick glasses, her big brown eyes were glistening.

Meanwhile, Yochie had been examining the second box. "And this is a printer," she said. She turned to her sister. "Oh, Tikva, this is so exciting!" Her eyes, too, were wet.

Mr. Baker cleared his throat. "These six buttons," he said, pointing to the keyboard which rested in Tikva's hands, "correspond to the six points of which braille letters are made up. The other buttons are self-explanatory. The really fascinating part is this ribbon below the space bar. Behind the ribbon are pins, which poke holes in the ribbon, creating the bumps of the braille. This keyboard can read the screen, one line at a time, and 'print' it on the ribbon, therefore enabling the sight-impaired person to 'see' what's on the screen."

"Wow! Is this ever neat!" Moishy cried.

"Let's hook it up, shall we?" Mr. Baker started to unpack the printer.

Quite a while later, with many suggestions from Moishy and not a few from the other children, the keyboard and printer were ready to go.

"I still think you should have..." Moishy began.

"Oh, Moishy, enough is enough," interrupted Dini. "Abba knows what he's doing. He probably could have invented this machine!"

"Not quite," Mr. Baker chuckled. "Not quite. Come, Tikva. Let's see if it works."

Tikva had been very quiet while the family was connecting the keyboard and printer. Now, hesitantly, she took her place at the desk. She turned on the computer and loaded the program that came with the keyboard.

Then she began to type. "Welcome to Baker Campaign Headquarters" appeared on the screen. She ran her fingers across the silver ribbon. "That's just what it says here," she said wonderingly. She instructed the computer to print. She tore off the sheet and ran her fingers over the bumps on the page. "And here, too!"

She turned back to the keyboard and typed another sentence. "Thank you, Abba. I love you" appeared on the screen.

Mr. Baker lightly ran his fingers across the silver tape. Then he reached out for his daughter and gently embraced her. A tear ran down his cheek. "I love you too, Tikki," he said. "*Baruch Hashem*, I love you too."

14
And the Winner Is...

The phone rang. Donny ran to answer it. "Abba, it's for you!"

"It must be campaign headquarters," said Mr. Baker as he went to get the phone. "Baker here."

"Maybe they have news about the election results!" Moishy exclaimed. Clustering around their father, all the children began speculating in excited tones.

Mr. Baker raised his voice. "What was that? Excuse me? I can't.... Wait, just one moment, please." Mr. Baker placed a hand over the receiver. "Shhhh! Please, I can't hear."

"Come," Mrs. Baker whispered. She led the way out of the study. The family filed out after her.

Back in the living room, everyone restocked their

plates while keeping one eye on the study door for the first glimpse of Mr. Baker's return.

Mrs. Baker leaned back on the couch, the baby in her arms. Rachel Ahuva sucked noisily on an oversized pretzel.

"Anyone have any interesting school news today?"

"Chaim Oberlander lost a front tooth," Donny offered.

"Did he?" said Mrs. Baker. "He's young for that."

"He's the biggest in Donny's class," cut in Yochie. "Say, Moishy, aren't you learning with his brother?"

Moishy shrank visibly into the sofa cushions. He was saved from answering by Mr. Baker's return to the living room.

"It's close, my dears — very close." He sank into a chair.

"How close?" asked Ashi.

"Very close!" answered Mr. Baker. "Let's not talk about it any more."

"How can you not talk about it?" Zahava was shrill.

Mr. Baker finished refilling his plate. "Like this," he said, taking a bite of potato chip. He turned to Moishy. "When are they giving out the M.V.B. award, Moishy?"

"Yeah!" Chezky clamored. "When will you get your award already?"

Moishy turned pale; then, as he spoke, his cheeks flushed. "They announced the winner today," he mumbled, staring hard at the floor.

"Yay!" Chezky tore off a yell.

"What's up, Moishy?" Mr. Baker looked at his downcast child.

Moishy was quiet for a moment. Then he spoke, in a low, quavering voice. "Berel Oberlander won." Against his will his eyes brimmed with tears. His brothers and sisters gaped at him.

Chezky was the first to speak. "What? Berel Oberlander? But *you* were supposed to win. You're the smartest kid in the class, not him!"

"Hush, Chezky," said Mrs. Baker.

"But Ima, Moishy was supposed to win! They ought to do a recount, or something." Chezky crossed his arms and stood his ground.

"Hush, Chezky," said Mr. Baker. He turned to Moishy. "Do you think the decision wasn't correct? Do you feel shortchanged?" he asked quietly.

Moishy struggled for composure. He shook his head and sniffed. When he could talk again, he said, "It's like what you said, Abba, about working and finding. I guess Berel worked a lot harder than me. And he found...." Again his eyes threatened to spill over.

"But you spent hours and hours with those *mishnayos*!" protested Yochie.

"Yeah!" said Chezky.

"Well, Moishy?" asked Mr. Baker.

Moishy sighed. "I didn't understand. I guess I didn't want to understand. I just got carried away with... pride. *Mishnayos* are important, real important, but I guess to be 'valuable' you can't only learn *mishnayos*. And you can't let your other learning go bad to concentrate on one thing." Moishy paused. "When Berel improved all around, he gave to the whole class. When I learned *mishnayos*, I was giving only to myself." He looked up at his father.

Mr. Baker smiled at him. "Good boy, Moishy," he said. "I'm proud of you." He gave him a hug.

Mrs. Baker came over and hugged him, too. "I think this month you're the Bakers' Most Valuable *Bochur*."

"That was beautiful, Moishy," said Bracha. She hugged him, too. Moishy bore the embrace stoically. But when the quints wanted to hug him, too, he firmly fended them off.

"Enough is enough," he said. He grinned weakly. "If I'm too valuable, you won't be able to keep me!"

"Well, I'm glad to see your sense of humor's back," said Ashi as he laughed.

"*You* try a quintuplet hug!" Moishy shuddered.

"Let's get him!" shouted Yochie, lunging. Rivka grabbed her arm. But before Yochie could react, the phone rang. Zahava jumped. "The phone, Abba!"

Mr. Baker nodded and went to the phone. Mrs. Baker and the children waited in tense silence. He spoke briefly, thanked the caller, and hung up. Not a sound was heard as he turned slowly to face his family.

"Well, kids, this is it. They'll be announcing the official results in five minutes. The next time the phone rings, we'll know!"

"I just can't take it anymore," said Zahava, clutching at her hair with both hands. "What if Abba loses?"

"If I lose, I lose," said Mr. Baker philosophically.

"How can you say that?"

"What if I lose? I did my best. It was a lot of work and, I have to say, a very interesting experience. If I lose, I'll find other ways of contributing to the community. And don't forget, kids, if I lose I'll have more time to spend with you."

Moishy's face lit up. Bracha's eyes twinkled a little. Donny bounced up and climbed onto his father's lap. After a short tickle fight, he snuggled happily in Mr. Baker's arms.

"Abba?" Donny asked.

"What is it, Donny?"

"Is it okay to say Tehillim?"

Mr. Baker was taken aback. "Why, sure, Donny. It's always okay to say Tehillim. Somehow I never pictured praying for an election result — though when I was a kid I had a friend who davened for the Yankees." Everyone laughed. "I picture Tehillim for someone who is sick or something like that. My winning this election isn't all that important."

"You don't understand, Abba," Donny grinned up at him. "I want to daven that you *lose*!"

Mr. Baker's mouth opened in an "Oh." Mrs. Baker tried hard not to laugh; she wasn't very successful. Soon everyone was laughing, including Mr. Baker.

The phone rang.

The laughter stopped suddenly, like turning off a switch. In the stillness after the noise died, Dini could hear every tick of the antique clock on their old piano. Mr. Baker swallowed hard and went to answer it.

The children barely breathed. Mr. Baker spoke into the phone. "Yes. Yes, I see.... Yes, thank you. Good night." He hung up the phone and went back to the family group.

"Well, gang, it was close, very close...but we lost." He looked first at his wife, and then at the children.

"I'm sorry, dear," said Mrs. Baker softly.

"Wow, poor Abba," said Bracha.

"That's tough, Abba," said Ashi. He offered his hand to his father. "But it was a job well done."

"Those people don't know what they're missing," Zahava burst out loyally. The other quints agreed vociferously.

Chezky sat on the couch, arms crossed, and muttered, "First Moishy, then Abba!"

Mr. Baker sat down next to him. Donny and Saraleh climbed on his lap. "It's all right, Chezky." He extricated a hand and patted Chezky on the shoulder.

"I'm glad!" said Donny.

"Me too!" echoed Saraleh.

"You don't even know what you're talking about!" Yochie told her.

"Maybe I'm glad, too," said Mr. Baker slowly.

"It probably would have been a lot of extra work," Mrs. Baker said in a thoughtful voice. "You would have been very tired. And we would have seen a lot less of you." She threw a questioning glance at her husband.

"I don't really mind," said Bracha.

"Me neither," Rivka added stoutly.

"Not at all!" agreed Dini.

"It's for the best," said Tikva, nodding.

"Abba at home!" exclaimed Zahava.

"Baker at home, I'll tell you why!" was Yochie's gleeful cry.

"Yochie!"

Mr. Baker broke into a broad grin. "Break out another bottle of soda. Let's drink a *lechaim*! Baker's Dozen are going to celebrate!"

"Celebrate what?" asked Moishy.

"Their father's back home!"

"But Abba, you worked hard. Really hard," Moishy said earnestly. "Don't you feel bad that you worked, and you didn't find?"

"Find? Of course I found!"

"What did you find?"

"What did I find?" Mr. Baker echoed. Smiling broadly, he gestured with an exuberant sweep of his hand. "I found the greatest family a father could ever want!"

Coming Up Next In
BAKER'S DOZEN

Wow! A pre-Purim concert with Avi Shoham! Wouldn't it be fabulous if the Bakers could go hear their favorite entertainer? But the event has been sold out for months, and there's no way they can get tickets.

Or is there?

When the quints discover that their quiet classmate, Idy Bodner, is Avi Shoham's first cousin, they begin a "Be Nice to Idy" campaign, hoping for free tickets. Instead, they wind up with a big mess!

The girls aren't the only ones with problems. Ashi has accused Moishy of never finishing anything he's begun. Moishy is determined to prove that he can see a project through to the end. But has he bitten off more than he can chew?

Join the Baker gang for more good fun — and important lessons — in *Stars in Their Eyes*.